A THOUSAND PERFECT NOTES

A

THOUSAND

PERFECT

NOTES

A THOUSAND PERFECT NOTES

C.G. DREWS

ORCHARD

ORCHARD BOOKS

First published in Great Britain in 2018 by The Watts Publishing Group

3 5 7 9 8 6 4 2

A CIP catalogue record for this book is available from the British Library.

ISBN 978 1 40834 990 8

Typeset in Sabon by Avon DataSet Ltd, Bidford-on-Avon,
Warwickshire

Printed and bound in Australia by McPherson's Printing Group

The paper and board used in this book are made from wood
from responsible sources.

Orchard Books
An imprint of Hachette Children's Group
Part of The Watts Publishing Group Limited
Carmelite House
50 Victoria Embankment
London EC4Y 0DZ

An Hachette UK Company
www.hachette.co.uk

www.hachettechildrens.co.uk

'You are worth more than a thousand perfect notes.'

CHAPTER 1

What he wants most in the world is to cut off his own hands.

At the wrist would be best. That hollow tiredness that stretches from fingertips to elbow would be gone for ever. How sick is that? There must be something seriously – dangerously – wrong if he can lie on his rock-solid mattress at night and think about lopping off limbs and using bloodied stumps to write 'HA!' on the walls. He'd be a scene out of a horror movie.

And he'd be free. Because, without hands, he's worthless to her.

To the Maestro.

His mother.

But the entire handless daydream would require *action* instead of *fantasising*, and he's not so good at that. Even stupid small stuff – like spontaneously detouring by an ice creamery on the way home from school and treating his little sister to a double whipped fudge cone instead of keeping the strict time schedule the Maestro demands – is impossible. He won't even try something like that. Why? A taste of fudge and freedom isn't worth it?

No.

He's just not made for rebellion or risks.

Fantasising is all he's good for. Sick dreams of mutilation, apparently. Which hand would he even cut off? Right? Or left?

It scares Beck Keverich – the way he thinks sometimes.

His digital clock reads 5:12. Still dark. Still cold. It's always easier to batter his way out of bed in summer, but now that autumn has wrapped bare, twiggy fingers around the universe, his alarm clock feels like it's shrieking in the middle of the night. And he should've been up twelve minutes ago.

It's surprising the Maestro hasn't rattled his door to roar at his laziness.

Beck peels his head off the pillows. He wishes he could dissolve into them. Did he even sleep last night? His wrists ache like he's been juggling blocks of cement. Did he quit at eleven? Midnight?

His fingers moan, *it was midnight, you fool*. They also say *get us warm* and *let us rest this morning* and even *we're going to curl into a fist and punch the wall until we shatter*. His fingers are cantankerous like that.

Beck rubs his hands together, blows on his numb fingers and curses broadly to the universe – because it's quicker than being specific about the depths of his loathing of the Maestro right now. Then he approaches the object of his doom, his life, his worth.

He slams the piano lid open.

The Steinway upright is the sole glory of his room. Not that there's much else *in* the room. He has a bed that feels like snuggling rocks, broken blinds on the windows, a wardrobe of second-hand clothes and shoes held together with duct tape and hope – and a twenty-thousand-dollar piano.

As the Maestro says, 'A good piano is all the hope I have that *mein Sohn* will improve his *schreckliche* music.'

Beck only spent his toddler years in Germany, but stayed bilingual by necessity – he needs to know when his mother is sprinkling burning insults over his head. Although her curled lips and glares also speak volumes.

Schreckliche means *terrible*. Awful.

It's a summary of Beck.

You are an awful pianist. Your music has no future. You have no talent. Why don't you play faster, better, clearer? Why do you hit the wrong notes all the time? Are you doing it on purpose areyouplayingbadlyonpurposeyouworthlesslittle—

'You suck, kid,' Beck says calmly to himself. 'So work.'

It's his routine pep talk to get motivated in the cold pre-dawn darkness. Now for staccato notes. Double fifth scales. Diminished seventh exercises. Fumbled notes. Trills for his iced fingers to fall across.

He'll wake the Maestro – although she's probably already awake and seething that he started late – and his little sister. He'll wake the neighbours, who hate him, and he'll start the local dogs howling. He'll shake the sleep from the weeds strangling the footpath, and the broken glass from some drunken brawl, and the homeless who lurk in the dank non-kid-friendly neighbourhood playground.

By 8 a.m. Beck's fingers will feel like flattened noodles and his eyelids will be coated in cement.

And all the time, he dreams of sawing off his hands or even his ears.

Of walking out and never coming back.

He dreams of utter silence – so then the tiny kernel of music inside him could be coaxed to life.

It's unbelievably noisy in his head, noisy with songs of his own creation. But since the Maestro will have none of it, it stays locked away.

Play the music on the paper. No one cares about the songs in your head.

His bedroom door crashes open and his little sister appears with a howl like a wildcat.

Joey is a tumbleweed of wire and jam stains, set on maximum speed and highest volume. She's exhausting just to *look* at.

'IT'S FIFTEEN MINUTES TILL WE GO,' Joey bellows. She solemnly believes Beck can't hear anything else when he's on the piano. He *can* hear, he just can't multitask and answer.

His cyclone of music fades and silence pours over Beck's fingers. Relief. By this point, if Chopin walked into the room, Beck would throttle him with a shoelace. He hates these pieces the Maestro demands he learn.

It's past eight. He's not even dressed or had breakfast.

'I hate Mondays,' he mutters and reaches for his school shirt. At least when one lives in a room the size of a broom closet everything is in easy reach.

Joey's face puckers. 'It's not Monday.'

'Every day is Monday.' A perpetual string of Mondays – he does belong in a horror film.

It takes his aching fingers two tries to get the buttons.

'I made you lunch,' Joey says, spider-climbing up his doorframe. 'A surprise lunch. A *scrumptious* surprise lunch.'

'That sounds ... terrifying.' Beck balls his holey pyjama shirt and throws it at her face. She gives an indignant squeak and drops from the walls.

To prove his point – OK, fine, because Joey loves a good show of theatrics – Beck drops to his knees, clasps his hands together, and wails like an impaled porpoise. She's giggling before he even starts to beg.

'Don't *punish me*. Please. What have I *done* to deserve this torment?'

'It's not torment!' Joey says, indignant. 'I'm a scrumptious cook. Even if you're a *bad brother* for being late yesterday.'

That would be on account of his English teacher, Mr Boyne, having a flare up of *I-care-about-your-horrible-grades-so-I'm-going-to-bawl-you-out-to-prove-it*, which included a demanded display of Beck's comprehension of the text. The 'comprehension' was, of course, non-existent. Hence Beck was late to pick up Joey.

The preschool teacher, whose face reminded him of a king crab, snapped at him about 'responsibilities', too.

'If I was a witch, I'd turn you into a toad,' Joey says, confidentially, ''cause everyone gets mad when we gotta go to the city for you, and Mama says we're going again soon.'

Beck cringes. There's a state championship coming up to obligingly stress everyone. Oh joy. And failure, with the Maestro hanging over his shoulder, is *not* an option.

'But I'd turn you back into a boy *someday*,' Joey says, warming up. ''Cause I like you, even if you always play the same notes over and over and over, because Mama says you're a *Schwachkopf*—'

Beck covers her mouth. 'OK, calm down. My delicate self-worth can only take so much. Is the Maestro already foaming at the mouth?'

Joey glares from behind his hand.

He removes it. 'I'm sorry I play the same song so much. I'm – practising. For that big concert.' *Practise, or the Maestro's fury will know no bounds.*

'Lean close,' Joey says, 'and I'll whisper *I forgive you* in your ear.'

Beck does without thinking. But she jumps on him, yowling like a kitten made of cacti, and Beck goes down in a tangle of shirtsleeves and mismatched buttons.

She's only his half-sister – the Maestro has an affinity for short relationships that end in screaming

7

fits and neither he nor Joey knew their fathers – but Joey's a pocketful of light in his gloomy existence. He has to love her twice as hard to make up for the sin of hating his mother.

Predictably, breakfast is cornflakes with a side dish of disapproval.

Has there ever been a time when the Maestro didn't greet him with a glare?

She sits in a corner of their tiny kitchen with squash-coloured décor that probably looked trendy thirty years ago. Who is Beck kidding? That shade of yellow *never* looked good. A single piece of burnt buttered toast sits next to her mug of coffee. The table can seat three, if no one minds bumping elbows, but as usual it's flooded with the Maestro's sheets of music. She tutors musicianship and theory at the university. Beck wonders how often her students cry.

Beck slinks past, telling himself he did everything right. She has nothing to erupt about. It'll be OK – totally OK.

He reaches for two bowls as Joey bangs around his legs, prattling about how she's going to be a chef when she grows up.

'And I'm gonna call my restaurant –' she sucks in a deep breath to yell '– JOEY'S GOODEST GRUB.' She jabs her spoon into Beck's ribs to get his attention. 'That's a great name, right?'

'Yow – *yes*.' He snatches the spoon off her.

He fills Joey's bowl with cornflakes first, which leaves him with the mostly smashed flake dust. With milk, it'll become sludge. Brilliant. He sets Joey's bowl on her pink plastic kiddie table in the corner, and eats his while leaning on the fridge.

Joey launches into a detailed description of what her chef apron will look like – something about it being shaped like a unicorn – which exactly no one listens to.

Beck watches the Maestro's red pen whip over the music. The students' work looks like something has been murdered over it.

Beck checks the plastic bag with his squashed sandwich. Joey has a thing about making his lunch. He sniffs it and detects peanut butter, tomato sauce and – are those raw pasta shells? Maybe he'd rather not know.

'You'll be late.' The Maestro's voice is deep and raspy. Even if she didn't have the temperament of a bull, she's an intimidating-looking woman. Broad-shouldered, six foot, with a crop of wiry black hair like a bristle brush – and she has long, spider-like fingers born for the piano.

Beck shovels the last globs of cornflake sludge into his mouth and then runs for the school bags. He crams in his untouched homework and sandwich, but takes more time with Joey's –

checking that she has a clean change of clothes in there, that her gumboots are dry, and her rainbow jacket isn't too filthy. A finger-comb through his curly hair and duct-taped shoes on his feet, and he's ready.

Joey pops out of her bedroom dressed in overalls with a pink beanie over her brush-resistant black curls. She snatches her jacket off Beck and dances towards the door. Preschool is blissfully free of dress regulations.

Beck has worn the same uniform shirt for so long it looks more pink than red.

They're about to run for the front door when the Maestro shuffles papers and says, 'A word, *mein Sohn.*'

Really? They have to do this now? She couldn't just let them skid out of the door, out of her hair, without raking him over the hot coals for once?

Joey kicks the front door open with her glittered gumboots. 'I'm gonna beat you there!' she yells.

Beck slinks back into the kitchen, slowly, his eyes on the ugly tiled floor. If he doesn't make eye contact with the tiger, it won't eat him, right? One of these days he'll just bolt out the door, defy her, just once. Instead of acting the obedient puppy, resigned to its next kick.

'*Ja, Mutter?*' He uses German as a tentative appeasement.

The Maestro lays down the red pen and kneads her knotted fingers. The tremors have already started for the day – the tremors that destroyed her career and turned her into a tornado over Beck's.

Painfully slow seconds tick by like swats against Beck's face.

He has to get out.

Needs

to

leave.

'You woke late,' the Maestro says. 'I don't permit *Faulheit* in my house.'

'I didn't mean to be lazy.' Yeah, he slept in all of twelve minutes. 'I'm sorry.' Suck up. It's the only way to get out alive.

The Maestro snorts. 'Why are you inept at dedication and commitment? Do you want your progress to stagnate?' She picks up her mug. It trembles violently and coffee sloshes over the side. 'Or is this your streak of *teenage* rebellion?' She sneers the word 'teenage', like she never was one. Which is highly likely. Beck always imagines she strode into the world as a bitter giant, ready to clobber everyone with a piano.

'I'm sorry.' Beck resists a glance at the front door to see how far Joey's gone. He doesn't like her to cross the road alone.

'*Ja*, of course you are sorry. A little parrot with

only one phrase to say. A lazy parrot who – *look at me* when I speak to you.' Her crunchy voice rises, and she hauls herself upright, more coffee escaping her mug and dripping down her wrist.

He doesn't want to do this again. He's going to be *late.*

'*Mutter*, please, I've got school.' Beck snatches a glance at the clock.

Her hand flashes out of nowhere and slaps his face. The shock of it sends him a step backwards. He always forgets how fast she can move.

'Do not disrespect me!' she snaps. 'School is not important. I am speaking to you. *That* is important.'

Beck does nothing.

'The only important thing in your life is the piano.' Her voice shakes the ceiling plaster. 'The piano *is* life. And every time you laze instead of practising, you shame me. You shame my name. You'll amount to nothing, *Sohn*, nothing! Are you listening?'

'Yes, *Mutter*.' Beck speaks to his shoes.

'Is my advice a joke to you? LOOK AT ME WHEN I SPEAK.'

Beck's neck snaps straight to stare into her angry eyes – and she tosses her coffee straight in his face.

There's a petrifying moment when he thinks it'll be hot, that it'll scald the skin off his bones. But it's

12

lukewarm. Coffee slides down his face and soaks his hair, his shirt collar.

Beck chokes on something – definitely not a whimper, possibly rage – and clenches his hands behind his back.

'Does this feel like a joke now?'

Beck refuses to wipe his face. He stands statue still and meets her eyes again. 'No.'

The Maestro lowers the empty mug, which is, Beck concedes, a positive movement since she didn't smash it across his skull to finalise the lesson.

'That is how it feels,' the Maestro says, 'when you throw the sacrifices I've made for you back in my face. Now go to school, *du Teufel*.'

You devil.

He doesn't ask to change his shirt – he's not going to stick around in case she changes her mind and flings the mug at his teeth – so he just nods and runs for the door. *Goodbye, Mother, thank you, Mother, what would I do without your helpful life advice, Mother*. He wants to hurt something. But all he can do is shut the front door, quietly, respectfully, and turn around and punch the brick wall.

But not too hard.

He can't bust his hand – or she'd really kill him.

Blood bubbles on his knuckles as he walks down the driveway and catches up with Joey, who's picking weeds and dandelions along the broken footpath.

'This is for my teacher,' Joey says proudly.

'I'm sure she'll love those affectionately picked weeds.' Beck flexes his hand: stupid, stupid, *stupid*. But he's pleased his voice stays level, kind. He'll never let anything affect how he treats and talks to Joey.

Joey wrinkles her nose. 'Why are you wet?'

Beck takes her hand in his bleeding one. 'It was just a joke,' he says.

CHAPTER 2

Maybe it is a joke, all of this.

His life.

This school.

This place.

Maybe if he just laughed it off, didn't let it touch him –

Stupid. Who is he kidding? It's never going to be different so why overthink it?

Beck would love to dump Joey at the preschool gate – drop and run – but he refuses to be that kind of big brother. Someone needs to walk her in, admire her cubbyhole decorated with sparkles and fruit stickers, and the nine art creations she forgot to take home. He always leaves with glitter on his hands. He's pretty sure glitter is an evil substance that is magnetically attracted to people who hate it most.

The trick is to get out before the preschool teacher pounces. She always suffocates Beck with questions he can't answer – Joey's lunchbox is unbalanced, where is her fruit; she needs proper playing shoes, gumboots are unacceptable; paperclips are *not* OK substitutes for hair clips; when is their mother going to pop in for a chat; Joey has been acting far too aggressive to the other kids; is everything OK at home?

Beck exits before the cat pounces. He doesn't want anyone to notice his damp shirt and coffee aura.

Is everything OK at home? Of course. His expensive piano is the reason his sister doesn't get fresh mandarins or meat in her sandwiches. His mother doesn't care to meet the teachers of her insufferable children. He's doing his best, OK?

He's late for his classes. Late, late, late. Which surprises exactly no one. But his school is where brain cells go to wither, where no one hands in homework, and half the class of fifteen-year-olds can barely read. No, really. He's not even the worst. He can get through the basics, laboriously, and while everyone else screws with the teachers, Beck writes music.

Mostly in his head. He sucks at notation. But closing his eyes, resting his chin on his arms and *creating*, is the only way he gets through a day.

He can't care about anything else. He can't.

The music in his head is his pocket of relief, the only thing he passionately cares about. Well, it and Joey. If he stretches to care about something else – like what the Maestro thinks of him or how he fails at school or what he really wants to do with his life – he'll be pulled too thin. His skin will part like old paper and the world will see how his skeleton is made of dark wishes and macabre dreams. They'll know his heart thumps to the beat of the Maestro's metronome because it's too scared to do otherwise.

But worst?

They'll see the emptiness inside him.

Being a pianist is stitched on his skin, but his bones are tattooed with whispers of *you fake, you fake*.

English is the worst class, because Mr Boyne refuses to give up on any student. He even makes Squinty Mike – the dude could get glasses and fix it, but, whatever – read aloud when the guy can't even spell his own *name*.

Beck doodles music notes over his worksheet and feels his pencil sink into the ruts on the desk. Someone's carved their opinion of school in four-letter words all over the lid. Their opinion isn't as disturbing as the fact they *had a knife in school*. Beck hopes the kid is graduated and *gone*. And probably in prison.

'... which will be quite a stretch for most of you,' Mr Boyne says. 'But that's why the pairing isn't random – no, Avery, there'll be no switching. And Chris, if you could possibly pretend this class is interesting enough to stay awake for, I'd be ever so obliged.'

Pairing? Group projects? Is the world intent on being cruel today? Beck was so busy being mentally absent that he has no idea what the project even *is*.

Mr Boyne strolls down the lines of desks, rattling off names. 'Move desks if you need to. Quietly. QUIETLY.'

Kids toss backpacks and books, noise escalating as they find their partners. Most are yelling questions or whining about their match.

'No swaps permitted, Ellen. No swa— no, no SWAPS. Everyone pause for a minute while I say NO SWAPS ARE HAPPENING. Yes, it applies to you, Avery.' Mr Boyne continues reading out names. 'Emeka and Abby. Stephanie and Noah. Ajeet and – I can't even read my own writing. Oh, Mike. Swap seats. Do it quietly. Do it *now*.'

Beck sweats.

Mr Boyne pauses in front of his desk and raises

an eyebrow at the lines of scrawled semiquavers and crotchet rests. 'Interested in my class as always, I see, Mr Keverich.'

Beck wishes he'd paid enough attention to know *why* he is being tied to someone and sentenced to death.

'Beck and August.' Mr Boyne strides past.

Beck purposefully doesn't take note of the other kids, so their names and faces are a tangled confusion to him. He's nothing like them. He has no phone, no internet, and he avoids sport in case he hurts his piano hands. And considering he's forever lost in his head, his music, they've given up speaking to him anyway.

Then there's the Maestro's rule: no friends, no distractions.

'The piano will make you great someday,' she always says, 'while a friend takes and takes and takes and leaves you with nothing.'

But as a tall, sun-kissed girl in a *Save The Whales* T-shirt appears in front of his desk, Beck knows exactly who she is.

August Frey.

She's the kind of girl who wears handmade shirts over the top of her school uniform and gives soliloquies on tree frogs – not that Beck's actually *heard* them, he's just heard *of them* – and has dirt-blonde hair and never wears shoes.

She grabs the vacated desk next to him and dumps her books, with actual notes on the assignment. Beck angles himself to peek, but her handwriting is tiny and cramped, and he's not so hot at reading sideways. Or front ways.

She gives him a small smile and Beck looks down. He's never sure how to react to kids in his class. If he smiles, they might think he's friendly, and then what? He'll have to wear a poster board that says, *If I ever make a friend my mother will noose me.*

Mr Boyne has finishing shuffling the seating and returns to the front of the class. He always wears a bow tie with small fruit patterns on it. Today is bananas. How fitting.

'All right, eyes to the front. Everyone listen up – which means you, Keverich.'

Beck blinks. Please don't expect him to use his brain. He's been up since five, hammering scales and arpeggios, and he'd kill for a nine-hour nap.

'Now,' Mr Boyne says, 'you've been paired according to abilities, or lack thereof. A student who is failing with a student who cares about succeeding.' He eyeballs everyone pointedly.

'But that's not fair!' someone wails.

'It's great motivation to work hard,' Mr Boyne says. 'Or harder. Or, for the first time this year, work at all. You're getting a chance to bump up your grades while being tutored. No one is allowed to squander this.'

Beck's mouth opens by accident. Definitely an accident. Since when does he speak up in class?

'But to be failing,' he says, 'means we're trying in the first place.'

Snickers. A dark look from Mr Boyne. A curious one from his English partner-to-be.

'Anyone with something smart to say gets a visit to the principal's office.' Mr Boyne adjusts his bow tie. 'And then the principal will chat with your *parents*.'

Oh, how scary. As if any of their parents would care. Most of these kids are barely literate ghosts. Here one year, drifting off to work at McDonald's the next.

Except for Beck, of course. While they're fighting for a low-income job, he'll be a famous pianist.

Great.

Mr Boyne clears his throat as if expecting the class will settle. It doesn't. He raises his voice and rocks on his heels, like if he makes himself taller they'll pay attention. They won't.

'The goal, naturally, is the essay. It will need to be two thousand words – that's one thousand each – with detail, quotes and examples.'

Examples of *what*?

'It's due in two weeks, which is plenty of time to

get to know your partner. You can meet after school or – oh, organise that amongst yourselves.'

Wait, meet after school? That can't happen. Beck feels his world narrow in suffocation.

'Remember the subject! The essay must be a detailed comparison of two opposite opinions—'

'What if we agree on everything?' someone yells.

'Then get married,' Mr Boyne says without blinking.

The class giggles.

'You will find something,' Mr Boyne says, 'and keep in mind hobbies and interests are *not* allowed. You will be contrasting political, moral, or religious views. Present me a convincing point of view. Be respectful to your partners. Be intelligent.' He pauses and rubs his bow tie again. 'Be intelligent *if you can*.'

Mr Boyne seems to think that covers it. 'Now, we have ten minutes before the end of this period, so get to know your partner and start discussing topics for your contrast essay.' He plops behind his desk, apparently done with everyone and everything. For ever.

Beck has questions. Firstly, how is he going to find time to do this? After school? Come on! And secondly, contrast political opinions? He has no opinions. He has nothing but a piano and aching fingers.

August sweeps her hair over her shoulder and shoves her desk closer to his. She then sits on it, and rests her chin on her fist. The rest of the class has erupted into loud conversation – probably unproductive – but August seems curtained off in a bubble of quiet focus.

Focus directed at Beck.

This is so bad.

'Hi,' August says.

'Beck,' he says, then feels stupid because Mr Boyne bawled everyone's names across the class. She's going to *know*.

'What's that short for? Beckett?'

'Something like that.' His full name is a topic he'll never touch with anyone. Ever.

Did he mention *not ever*?

August's grin is like a sly wood nymph. Beck can't stop looking at her hand-printed T-shirt. How can she get away with that while he gets detention for tardiness?

'Wow, calm down,' August says. 'I'm overwhelmed with all the information you're throwing at me.'

Beck feels trapped. What does he say? 'This whole assignment is stupid.' Wait. Did he say that out loud?

'I won't disagree.' August tilts forward on the desk top. Her hands are covered in blue Sharpie doodles and her eyes are as complicated as the ocean. Beck decides to avoid looking at them. She whips out an orange Sharpie and she taps it on his desk. 'How do you feel about tattoos?'

'How is that political?' Beck says.

'Moral.' August uncaps the lid and adds a swirl. The orange is nearly lost against her deeply tanned skin. 'Some places won't hire you if you're tattooed.'

'That seems – wrong.'

August sighs. 'Agreed. And we're not supposed to agree. So your turn – suggest something, music boy.'

Beck freezes. How did she – she couldn't. He's never breathed a word about the piano to anyone and no one would even catch him with headphones. She couldn't possibly know about the piano. Unless ... He looks at his worksheet, doodled with music notes. He flips it over and flattens his blood-crusted hand over it.

'Did you punch someone on the way over?' August says.

If only.

'I'm not a *music boy*,' he says stiffly.

From the sounds the rest of the class is emitting, everyone else considers this a get-to-know-you party. Only half the kids have their phones out already.

'We could contrast our music tastes – that can be moral too.' August sprouts a green Sharpie. 'You know, how people think heavy metal is evil? Well, my dad does.' She gives a little snort. 'He was in a rock band when he was my age and now he does yoga to Brahms. What do you listen to?'

'Nothing.' He'd rather strangle himself with a piano string than tell her he's into classical. What kind of fifteen-year-old boy admits to being obsessed – by force or choice, it doesn't matter when it's his whole life – with classical music?

The bell roars and the class folds up in one motion, everyone grabbing bags and yelling out times to meet up on the weekend.

'Great,' August says. 'I practically know everything about you.'

Looking at her round face and sparkling eyes, Beck wouldn't have picked her for the caustic type. But he's hardly a judge of character.

'I'm sorry.' His voice comes out way too high, strangled. 'I can't – meet up, I mean. It's not going to work—'

'It's not optional.' August leans forward, bared Sharpie all too threatening. 'We have two weeks and I'm not failing an assignment because you're lazy.'

Lazy.

It must be true if the entire world agrees on it.

Beck tries to keep his face neutral. 'I have to walk my sister home. Then I –' *play the piano until my fingers bleed.*

August's eyes light up. 'I'll walk with you. I'm on Gully Avenue. Number eleven.'

And she lives so close. Seriously? Could the universe not cut him a break? He doesn't ask much.

'Thirty-two Dormer,' he mumbles.

'Awesome, we're practically neighbours. Well, give or take three blocks. You can pick whose house we invade—'

'I can't.'

August looks at him long, hard. It's like being frowned at by an entire ocean. But what choice does he have? The Maestro would—

He chooses not to envision her reaction to a classmate strolling into her house with an impish grin and bright eyes. August's eyes say she's never been let down in her entire life. Lucky her.

'Can I ask a question?' August's pen tap-taps on his desk.

The class empties around them.

He squirms, but it must look like a nod, because she says, 'Why do you smell like coffee?'

'I love it so much I wear it.'

August pokes his sticky cheek. He nearly flinches, *nearly*. Great, she has no personal boundaries.

'Fascinating. And you know what I love? Good

grades. I love them so much I wear them – no, really. I'm going to make a dress for the prom out of all my A plus report cards.' She clips the lid back on her Sharpie – relief, the weapon is shielded. 'And I'm willing to enable your fetish. I'll treat you to a cinnamon latte once this is done.'

'Bribes?' He's not sure he'll ever feel like a coffee after this morning. There's nothing like that sick dread of wondering if you're going to burn.

'You can even pour it over your head and I won't comment.' August smiles and Beck can't decide if it's sinister or friendly. Probably both. Simultaneously?

'Maybe during lunch,' Beck says. 'Or walking to and from school. But not after school because – I have a little sister. A preschooler.'

'You *keep* saying that,' August muses. 'Must be a high maintenance kid. Can't she watch TV while we type up an argument?'

'I smell an only child.'

August raises her hands in mock surrender. 'Caught me. I was such a perfect kid, my parents decided not to risk a secondary disaster.'

Beck has a sly comment about her being so *awful* they quit reproducing, but Mr Boyne looms over his desk, banana bow tie inches from Beck's nose. 'Don't you have lunchtime detention to get to, Mr Keverich?'

Beck gathers his papers and August snatches her backpack off the floor.

'Meet you at the preschool,' August says, and scoots out the door.

Beck's left with his mouth slightly open, his head spinning, and the realisation that she's not going to take rudeness as a no. He'd better try harder. Surely he can channel his inner Maestro and—

No.

He's always promised himself he'll be polite to anyone, everyone, to avoid being like the Maestro.

Mr Boyne claps a hand on Beck's shoulder. 'I think you two are going to have an interesting time.' He grins and then shoves Beck towards the door.

Interesting? Try *disaster*.

CHAPTER 3

If Beck gets to the preschool early –

If August forgets –

If the world ends –

But Beck has never been lucky, and, even after his bolting for the preschool at breakneck speed and hustling Joey out in record time, August Frey is waiting for them at the gate. 'Hey, Beck!' She waves broadly in case Beck forgot or something.

He wishes.

Joey spies August's lanky arms knotted over the fence and gives Beck's hand a sharp tug. 'How did you get a *girlfriend*, Beck?'

Beck is microscopically offended. 'What do you mean "how"?'

'Well, you're a boy and boys are gross,' Joey says.

Beck wrestles with the preschool gate – the childproof latch is also adultproof due to rust and lack of funding. 'She's not my girlfriend. She's – we're – it's for school. So don't yap all the way home, OK?'

But the second they're free of the preschool's boundaries, Joey snatches her hand free of Beck's and struts straight to August. 'Why are you Beck's girlfriend?'

He'd like to disappear right now.

For an only child, August is surprisingly not patronising to little kids. She doesn't squat or pat Joey's head. Instead she points to Joey's blue macaroni necklace and says, 'I like this.' She smirks at Beck. 'And I also like coffee and Beck just happens to smell like coffee, so I'm going to follow him home.'

Joey frowns. 'Oh, so that's why he tipped coffee on his head.'

Beck considers covering her mouth, except it'd earn him a kick. He adjusts his backpack straps and ploughs down the footpath, knowing Joey will follow and hoping August won't.

'Beck and I are working on a school project,' August says behind him.

Joey's gumboots slap on the uneven footpath.

'What project?'

'Project Make Beck Smile.'

Beck swivels, walking backwards, and smiles. 'Done. We can go our separate ways.'

'That was painful just to *watch*,' August says. 'You really ought to practise that at home. Alone. Where you can't terrify small children.'

'Ha ha.' Beck turns away. 'Seriously, we can work in class or – something. But not now. Bye.'

Joey breaks into a jog and catches Beck's hand. She rarely does that these days, since she's so Old and Capable, as she regularly informs him. Her whisper is a spittle-filled shout. 'Is she being mean to you? You're s'posed to tell mean people to go away.'

Beck shrugs. They've arrived at an intersection, so he checks for traffic – and then glances to see if August is still there.

He could've sworn the twitch on her lips was amusement.

'I'll help.' Joey clears her throat. 'Go away, *Schwachkopf*!'

'Whoa.' August raises an eyebrow. 'Did the *preschooler* just swear at me in German?'

'No, she only called you a moron.' Beck takes Joey's hand and charges across the road. 'That's unkind, Joey. Feel free to do it again.'

But August dashes after them and arrives on the

kerb with a bounce, as if no German insult could knock the smile from her lips. If only Beck was so resilient.

'So warm,' August says, 'so kind. It's lovely hanging out with the Keverichs.'

Imagine letting her meet his mother.

Discussion fades as they walk. August doesn't press possible topics for the essay, but she walks blithely, like she's hanging out with a real friend. Beck doesn't know how to handle this. He's done his best to scare her off without being *too* rude. But shouldn't acting like an icy jerk be enough?

As they cross the playground, littered with smashed beer bottles and homeless squatters, August informs them that she didn't know about this good shortcut home. If by 'good' she means 'utterly terrifying since who knows when someone's going to pop out a knife and demand money' then sure, Beck says she's welcome for the tip.

He feels embarrassment at his dumpy street where no lawns are mowed and the neighbour is growing marijuana amongst the eggplants – but then he's furious at himself. August lives around here *too*. She's no privileged snob. Who knows? Maybe her parents are weed-smoking hippies who are barely present in her life. He knows nothing about August.

And he'll keep it that way.

To be safe.

With a hoot, Joey dashes towards their sunken little house. One window is boarded, and the letterbox is a plastic bucket with a rock in it since someone actually stole theirs. Who steals letterboxes?

August peers at the house curiously as Joey wrenches open the door and disappears inside, hollering, 'I'M HOME!'

How does he say *goodbye-and-you're-never-coming-in?*

'Well, later then,' Beck says.

'Don't forget I'm at eleven Gully!' August says. 'If you want to drop by and work. Because you'd better believe we're going to ace this paper.'

'Yeah.' Beck kicks at the footpath where a slab of concrete is missing. 'I'm sorry, I – I am. But. It's just not going to work. I'm sorry about your mark, but Mr Boyne won't dock you if I suck.'

'Dude, you could get expelled. It's worth, like, half the grade.'

What she doesn't say is *and everyone knows you're failing already.*

'It doesn't matter.' The Maestro probably wouldn't even send him to a new school. He'd have eighteen hours a day to practise instead! Beck shudders. 'My family – my mum – it's complicated.'

'Oh.' Finally her eyes cloud and her smile slips.

Her grin is so comfortable, so easy, that when wrinkles cross her brow Beck feels like a monster. Cheerfulness is irritating, but it suits some people. Some people are born for sunlight and orange peel smiles and running on the beach and wild flowers in their hair.

Other people are born for nonexistence.

'So you're not actually *allowed* people over?' August says.

Beck is late for afternoon practice. And after this morning? This could be catastrophic. The Maestro isn't above taking out her frustration on Joey, to punish him. 'Something like that.' He wants to be invisible. An invisible boy with an invisible song in his head.

He turns, tugging at his backpack like a security blanket, and heads for the house. He doesn't look back. But he hopes her smile returns when he's gone, because it's a cruel person who steals smiles.

He's doing what his mother wants. *People change and betray you, but the piano does not.*

Ten minutes before the Maestro's bus is due and she'll descend with papers to correct and curses about unmusical idiots, Beck corners Joey for a loving brotherly threat session.

'You can't tell about August,' he says.

Joey sits in the middle of her floor, 'operating'

on her stuffed animals. They take up at least eighty per cent of her floor space – the rest is littered with coloured macaroni or ice-lolly-stick art.

'August, your girlfriend?' Joey pulls stuffing out of a tired-looking bear with her blue plastic doctor scissors.

'She's *not* my girlfriend.' If she doesn't stop obsessing about this, Beck is doomed. 'She's like … a friend.' If walking next to someone on the way home and insulting her counts as friendship. 'Like you hang out with Bailey.'

'I *don't* like Bailey any more,' Joey says stiffly. The poor bear gets an extra hard jab with the pretend needle. 'I'm never talking to that *Schwachkopf* again.'

He raises his hands in surrender. 'OK. Sorry. I didn't know. But, please, Jo, I'm begging. I'll do anything.'

'Can I have chocolate?'

Of course she had to ask for that. Where is he going to get chocolate? He doesn't even have money. 'OK, fine,' Beck says. 'I'll get you chocolate. So don't ever mention August's name.' He starts to leave and comes back. 'Or that you know a secret.' He hesitates. 'Or that I'm going to give you chocolate.'

Joey grins.

August is not his friend, no matter if he even

wanted one. They don't even know each other.

Beck is unknowable.

He disappears back into his room, dissolves into the piano. He has an entire folder of études to learn, and not just *any* études but the ones the Maestro grew up performing to international acclaim. It's especially torturous because he can't play them like she did. Yet she has it stuck in her mind that he must? And he has to be *better* than her? He has a suspicion that, since she can no longer play, her goal in life is to make *him* into *her* so the world doesn't forget Ida Magdalena Keverich's name and her genius playing.

Her dream is doomed to fail.

He plays like a fiend all afternoon despite the pain in his cracked knuckles. He even skips taking a shower since he's used to smelling like coffee now, even if the sticky hair is unpleasant. He'd rather nail the étude and not hear the Maestro complaining loudly about the lack of talent as she heats up fish fingers and boils frozen peas.

Notes.

Chords.

Scales.

He floods the house with music that shook the world a hundred years ago. His fingers knot over complicated patterns and his thumbs fail when he needs them most. But, the Maestro's wrath aside,

36

he owes it to the music to find perfection.

But he thinks about August.

What it'd be like to have a friend.

What it'd be like to encourage her smile of sunshine and lemonade instead of cutting it in half.

What if she'd never been rejected as bluntly as that before? What if she'd skipped through the universe, somehow oblivious to cruelty, and then *he* came along?

Stop *thinking* like this. She's not Joey. She's his age and goes to the worst school in the state and can't be oblivious to disappointments. Life would be unbalanced without sharp words to stick in your ribs like a thousand little knives. Beck's here to fill the quota.

His fingers fall over the étude and he curses the piano. Curses himself.

He slams the keys and they howl with Chopin's chaos instead of his own.

CHAPTER 4

Awake at five.

Playing music until eight.

Kitchen smells of coffee and threats.

He cradles a cereal bowl in aching fingers.

Stay quiet and the dragon won't wake.

Hate everything recreationally.

Beck thinks August has reopened a raw rift of
bitterness. It's easy to drag himself through life
with his eyes closed and accept the hate – until
someone bumps him and forces him to look up
and realise life's cutting him with broken shards
while everyone else is dancing. It's suffocating. It's
unfair.

Joey perches on the bench making sandwiches

and wearing a dress-up chef hat and an apron that says *Kill The Cook* – Beck swore to her it said *Kiss* The Cook, but when she's older he'll be in trouble. She has creamed corn, stale crackers and a lot of mayonnaise.

'Thanks, Joey.' He wraps both sandwiches in tin foil and tries not to think about it.

'You're welcome, *Schwachkopf*,' she says cheerfully.

There's bitterness knowing the only reason she uses those insults and curses is because the Maestro yells them at Beck. If he played better, Joey wouldn't be a parrot, squawking lines of acid and knives.

'When I'm a chef,' Joey announces, 'I'm going to have a big pink knife. Like, a *massive one*.' She makes a chopping motion. 'Then I'll cut things up. BAM.'

'What about a pink spoon?' Beck says. 'Or a pink whisk?'

Joey gives him a *you're-an-idiot-why-do-I-have-to-put-up-with-you* look. 'Can you cut things up with a whisk, *Schwachkopf*? I want a knife.'

Of course she does. Tiny, scary, violent child.

Beck wonders if he ever juggled What I Want To Be When I Grow Up fantasies at her age. All he can remember is the piano. Sitting on the Maestro's lap – back when her hands didn't shake – as she guided his baby fingers up and down scales. When he was Joey's age, he was already the piano's barnacle. But Joey gets a childhood. She is the baby, the sweetheart. And currently it's more lucrative to threaten an oblivious Joey to make Beck work harder.

Or maybe the Maestro will inflict the piano on her too, someday.

Beck wishes he could do something. Protect Joey? Save her? But he's so pathetic he can't even buy her chocolate, or a proper birthday present, or even tell her that he hates it when she calls him *Schwachkopf*.

He's spineless.

They're about to leave for school in a blast of autumn air when the Maestro calls. Beck grinds his teeth. He practised from 5:03. She has nothing to yell about this morning.

Unless Joey let slip about August …

She promised.

She's *five years old*.

Beck drags himself back to the kitchen. He wonders how hot her coffee is.

'*Ja, Mutter?*' he says, weary.

The Maestro is in her routine place at the table, red-blotted papers spread before her. Purple smudges beneath her eyes say she's not sleeping well – but who can in this house, with the piano going all hours?

'I have some tutoring going late,' she says in German. 'Don't loiter on the way home. Come back and practise immediately.'

Beck breathes out and a thousand pieces of dread roll off his shoulders. '*Ja, Mutter*, of course.'

He's out the front door before she realises she didn't criticise his morning playing. The door slams behind him and he yells at Joey to wait for him – she's taken off already but is also wearing a necklace of Christmas bells, so locating her isn't hard – when it hits him.

How wrong everything feels.

How wrong it's about to become.

August Frey has been sitting in the gutter on the opposite side of the street. She springs to her feet like she ate crickets for breakfast and waves. What is she doing here? Is she *messing* with him? She's not wearing shoes, just blue hemp anklets and Sharpie doodles on her feet.

She doesn't belong on this street. She doesn't belong in his life.

Beck's eyes snap away and he charges up the street, a breath away from running. He snatches Joey's hand and practically knocks her over in an effort to walk faster.

August catches up with a skip and a bounce. 'Good morning, antisocial Keverichs!'

She's not going to give up, is she?

Beck mumbles something like *hello* and glares at the ground.

August falls into step beside him, a disconcerting spring in each step. At least she wears her uniform like a (semi) normal student, her red polo shirt making Beck's look pinker than usual.

Beck only slows the pace when they've rounded the corner and there's no possible way the Maestro will see them. Not that she's in the habit of peeping out the window to be sure they get off safely. Between the hours of 9 a.m. and 3 p.m., they are none of her concern.

'And I thought *I* was a fast walker,' August says lightly. 'You're so odd, you make me look normal.'

He bets neither of them have even *tasted* normal in their entire lives. Beck is so beyond normal he can't even focus on the fact that he has a pretty girl determined to hang around him.

Pretty? Well, she sort of is. She has freckles and those oceanic eyes and she looks like she could beat an Olympian in a sprint. Not the perfect hair kind of pretty or even the clean and tidy kind of pretty ... she's just—

Oh great. He's analysing what counts as *pretty*? This needs to stop.

'We can't talk to you,' Joey says.

August doesn't look surprised, or even offended

– more like she swallowed a smile and is trying not to let it escape. 'Why?'

Joey squints. 'You're a stranger?'

Beck could hug her. 'Be firm.'

'YOU'RE A STRANGER,' Joey yells and then looks pleased.

'I'm hardly stranger than you two,' August says. 'Plus you know my name, you know where I live, you know my favourite colour, and we hung out yesterday afternoon.'

'I don't know your favourite colour,' Joey says indignantly.

'It's blue.' Beck says it without thinking and then blushes dark enough to make a beetroot proud.

August meets his eyes with a smirk on the corner of her lips. 'Trophy for Keverich. What gave me away?'

The blue anklets and blue doodles on her feet and blue wool twined around some of her hair.

'Random guess,' Beck says.

Joey jerks her hand free to run a few metres ahead and leaps over a huge crack in the cement. She lands with a thump and her bell necklace clangs.

August moves ever so slightly closer to Beck. 'You don't smell like coffee today.'

'I've come to realise I hate coffee.'

'Then my bribe isn't going to work, is it?' August jiggles her satchel. 'I have a mango. Totally unseasonal mango and probably imported *but* I'm willing to share.'

Only one more block and they're at school. She makes him so uncomfortable.

'I'm not taking your mango,' he says. 'We're not friends.'

'We're not,' August agrees, 'we're essay partners. I want good grades and you don't want to get expelled.'

'Why don't you just ask Mr Boyne to swap you? With someone who cares?'

August presses her lips together. 'You say you don't care, but your eyes say differently.'

His *eyes*?

'Dude,' August says, 'your eyes have this permanent devastated look, like someone stole your ice cream *and* stabbed your puppy *and* then told you sprinkles were illegal. Your eyes clearly say they want to pass this assignment.'

They're at the school gate and Beck has never been so glad to see it. He could hug the broken wire fence right now. Being with August is like a hurricane of confusing emotions.

'Maybe sprinkles *are* illegal,' Beck says, 'and no one's told you yet.' He grabs Joey's hand and drags her towards the preschool.

Amongst the clamour of hundreds of kids elbowing their way to class, August shouts, 'I'll see you after school!'

Beck walks faster.

The high, primary and preschool are all squashed into two massive buildings. They're old. The air conditioners never work, so forget about heating. Most of the bathroom doors don't lock, if they're lucky enough to *have* a door. There isn't even a covered eating area, so rain or shine, kids wander about the sports oval and leave muesli bar wrappers everywhere they go. It's a dump. Beck feels sick dread for when Joey graduates to primary school and has to face these horrors.

He leaves her behind the safe, high fences – covered in rainbow streamers – of the preschool and trudges to class.

While the teachers drone about maths or biology, Beck writes music. His pencil squeaks a vicious storm – but it doesn't block out August.

She's going to be sticky about this, isn't she? And it's not just the assignment; she seems hell-bent on prying into the rest of his life. Maybe she thinks he's interesting? He's tried to be unremarkable. But if she found out about the piano or the reasons behind his bruises or the Maestro in general and *told* people – he can't even think about it. He'd be so embarrassed. What kind of fifteen-year-old guy is scared of his *mother*?

Beck tries to approach Mr Boyne – even though he has a strict no-teacher-contact policy – about changing partners to someone who doesn't care about school, but Mr Boyne waves him away.

'August is great. You'll be fine.'

'That isn't what I—'

But Mr Boyne flaps off to accost a student stealing whiteboard markers.

Can nothing in his *gottverdammten Leben* go right, for once?

Even getting Joey out fast fails because her teacher corners Beck to give a disapproving analysis of Joey's recent violent behaviour and how unacceptable it is. Beck has only just wriggled free of that when he realises Joey's made a robot costume out of boxes and they have a long, heated argument about the fact that she *can't* take it home. She howls at him for a few minutes and then goes boneless so he has to carry her out, which douses any notion of getting away before August can catch up.

August swings on the fence, a little less bouncy than usual.

'Why is your foot bleeding?' Joey demands.

'I kicked someone.' August gives a wan smile.

Beck hauls Joey up for a piggyback ride and tries to balance his backpack on one shoulder and hers on his other. He really doesn't have time to focus on August's freaking feet.

August reaches for his bag. 'I can carry—'

'I'm fine,' he says sharply.

She pulls back and he asks himself, for the millionth time, why he's such a devil. But it *has* to be this way. If *she* goes to Mr Boyne for a new partner, she'll get her way. He just has to suck enough to drive her to it.

August limps – unusually quiet – a few steps behind them. Good, maybe he can lose her.

But Beck finds himself walking slower and slower and then finally turns back to see how bad it is.

She's leaving bloodied footprints.

'*Meine Güte*,' Beck says sharply. 'You could've said you were dying.'

August stops and looks down. Her face is paler than usual, freckles sticking out, and she winces every time she steps.

Beck drops Joey on her feet and dumps his packs on the sidewalk. He's a jerk, yes, but he's not the kind of jerk that's going to let someone bleed to death.

'Do you have a phone?' August says weakly. 'I could call my dad to pick me up.'

Beck hesitates. 'Um, no. You don't have one?' Because he sure doesn't.

August shrugs. 'My family doesn't really believe in them. I mean, we're not living in a *cave*.' She lets out a half-hearted laugh. 'I have an iPod and we've got houselines and – sorry, I'm totally rambling.'

Beck tries to think if he has something in his bag he could wrap it in. His maths homework?

Joey creeps closer and squats in front of the battered foot. 'What did you kick?'

'*Who*, not what,' August says. 'Some idiot killing frogs in the guys' toilets.'

'You went into the boy toilets?' Joey draws back, as if this kind of idiocy is contagious.

August shrugs and sits down in the middle of the sidewalk. She cradles her bloody foot – it looks like a complete toenail is missing. 'You shouldn't kill things. Not dreams or happiness or animals. I'm really anti-killing. So the disagreement got a little physical and some guy had a stupid steel-toe boot and—' She bites her lip. 'I think I might've deflected off him into the wall.'

'You could wear shoes, you know.' Beck is desperately trying to think of a way he won't have to whip off his shirt and offer it as a bandage. Because – please no.

August grits her teeth. 'I knew you'd say that. But you know what? I shouldn't have to wear shoes to *kick* someone because they're killing harmless frogs.' Her face has gone red with the injustice.

'OK, whatever.' Beck turns around and squats down. He shrugs his shoulders. 'Get on my back.'

'What?'

Joey lets out a squeak of delight. 'Oh, Beck's gonna give you a piggyback!'

August eyes widen. 'Beck, I'm way too heavy ...'

'Nope.' Beck shrugs his shoulders again. 'Get on. I lift weights, you know.' He does not. 'I'm not leaving you to bleed to death on the sidewalk.'

'And here I was thinking that'd make you happy.' She peels herself off the footpath and hops towards Beck. 'I can call my dad from your house.'

And the Maestro won't be in till late – what a relief.

August touches his shoulders tentatively and then, with an 'I'm probably going to kill you,' she's on. Beck stumbles upright, stretches, and then hooks his arms under her thighs for balance. He's holding a girl. Her arms lie loosely around his throat. The smell of her is all over him – part sweat and coppery blood and coconut. She's no featherweight Joey, obviously, but he won't drop her.

He's got this.

He takes a step and then another.

Joey has picked up his backpack and has a look of severe concentration on her face as she trots

49

doggedly after them.

'Aren't I great?' August says dully. 'A damsel in distress.'

'Well,' Beck says, unwilling to admit to her – or himself – that he doesn't mind at *all*. 'When I kick a wall, you can carry me home.'

'Deal.'

Joey breaks into a jog to catch up, panting. 'I'm gonna kick a wall too!'

Beck groans. 'Oh, Joey, you *Schwachkopf*. I'll carry you tomorrow, I swear.'

Although August doesn't feel like an elephant on his back, Beck's knees still go slightly weak when he reaches his driveway. She slides off and, hanging off his elbow, she hops to the front door. Beck tackles it open with the key and holds his breath for a second, praying desperately that the house is empty.

Because what if it's not?

Hey, Mutter, *here's a bleeding girl I found who's possibly a friend? But I don't know. Jury's out. Don't kill me when she's gone.*

'Um, come in, I guess?' Beck holds the door open. He's never done this, not once in his life.

'I'll try not to bleed all over your house.' August limps inside after Joey.

Beck is having a small heart attack. So what does he do first? Does he give her the phone? Offer to bandage her foot? Give her some water? There's no food to offer, unless she wants cereal, and –

She's going to see how bare the house is. How cold. How bleak. They don't own much, just useful furniture and filing cabinets of music. No decorations. His family collects bruises and German insults instead of crockery and photo frames.

'This is the kitchen.' Joey guides August down the hall and into the tiny yellow kitchen. She pulls up a chair – at least the preschooler has manners, sort of … when she's not swearing at someone – and then she stands back and stares at August seriously. 'Do you need a Band-Aid?'

August raises her foot and surveys it. 'Probably a *big* Band-Aid.' Her soles are black with dirt and the blood has mixed with the grime so it's impossible to see the extent of the injury.

Beck gives her their house phone. His hands are shaking – *stupid, stupid*. But he can't quell the urge to do a quick dash around the house and check each room, each corner, to be sure the Maestro isn't here.

He abandons August to make the call and gets Joey a snack – a cup of milk and two biscuits – and gets her settled in front of the TV for the afternoon programmes. When he inches back into the kitchen, August hoists herself off the chair.

'He'll be here in a minute, so I'll wait on the driveway.'

'Oh, yeah, of course.'

He follows her out, feeling like an idiot but filled with the crushing need to be polite. He can't leave a bleeding girl alone on the sidewalk. But he doesn't want to meet her dad. He just wants to hide.

He should be at the piano.

What if the Maestro comes home early—

Stop.

They sit in the gutter, August cradling her damaged foot again, poking at it and emitting little hisses, and Beck holding her satchel.

'Contrary to your scowls and German insults,' August says, 'you're a bit of an angel.'

First time he's been called *that*.

Beck shrugs.

A rattling blue station wagon pulls up on the opposite side of the street. The driver window is down and a man with long hair leans out and waves.

August reaches over and punches his arm lightly. 'Thanks, Beck. By the way, what *is* your full name?'

He narrows his eyes. 'I think your ride is waiting.'

'OK, I'm totally getting to the bottom of that story someday.' She takes her satchel off him and limps across the road. She waves over her shoulder, but Beck is already escaping inside.

Close the door.

Have a solid barrier between himself and the world.

Remember what it felt like to carry August.

Never ever forget that.

Ugh, what is *wrong* with him?

Beck sentences himself to the piano. He doesn't even change from his uniform or make a snack – he just plays hard and fast. But he can't focus on études. All he can think of is how he carried August. And possibly ruined all passive-aggressive attempts to get her to hate him.

The Maestro thunders into the house at dusk.

From the way she bangs the cupboards in the kitchen and slams the kettle on, Beck decides not to venture out. At all.

But she comes in.

Her hands are trembling badly tonight and even clenching them in fists doesn't cover how viciously they shake. 'I expect you had a full afternoon practice?' she snaps, like he's already wronged her.

Beck breaks off in the middle of a scale. '*Ja.*'

'Good.' She grabs his doorframe, to steady herself or her shaking hands he doesn't know. But she's freaking him out.

'Are you – OK?'

'*Schwachkopf.*' The Maestro's lips pull back – in a smile? Beck feels like a small mouse a cat has decided to lunch on. 'Did you tell your teachers you'd be absent tomorrow?'

What?

Panicked, Beck stands, unsure if he should run because she's about to slap him into the middle of next week, or risk asking—

The confusion must've been too plain on his face, because the Maestro lets out a long-suffering sigh. 'The championship? The one we have been training for all year.' Her lips curl in a sneer. 'Did you forget, *Schwachkopf?*'

'*Nein,*' Beck says. 'I've been practising for it.'

He didn't forget. August just – distracted him for a moment. And that's proof of why he can't have friends.

If he were a piano, all his strings would have snapped.

CHAPTER 5

The terror isn't the performance – it's the aftermath with the Maestro.

She's unforgiving over a mistake. But worse? A flawless piece doesn't earn congratulations or celebratory ice cream. Instead there's depressing and crisp instructions on how he *still needs to improve*.

Maybe if the Maestro says 'you did well', the entire world would explode.

But even though Beck hates performing, there are, at least, small benefits. Odds are another contestant will wish him luck, a judge will shake his hand, there'll be a whisper of 'impressive' and 'that's talent to watch out for', which Beck knows is a lie – the Maestro keeps him grounded in the truth of failure – but is *nice* to hear all the same. Nice, because as much as he pretends to hate music, it's part of him. It *is* him.

He's done a thousand contests and concerts and exams and lessons. He knows how it plays out.

He always gets nervous.

It's all the people. The rows of a million eyes.

And how the Maestro will react afterwards.

The concert hall is jammed with tuxedos and formal wear and the haze of a thousand perfumes. Voices blur, hundreds at a time, and Beck fairly feels the sound of them. Tonight has been sponsored so thoroughly it's hosted in the City Concert Hall. Since the Keverichs live in the suburbs, it took nearly four hours to get into the heart of the city. Four hours in buses and trains, trying desperately not to sweat too much in formal wear. Four hours of the Maestro's glare. Four hours of Joey singing 'Incy Wincy Spider'.

All so Beck can compete in the championship for Best Young Pianist of the State.

He's not the best. He'll get a clap on the shoulder, a smile from a judge, the audience's admiration – but he won't win. He never does. What is the point of being here?

Beck stands in the behind-the-stage performance waiting area. When the stagehands move the huge purple curtains, he glimpses the blasting light, the sea of audience, the flash of the shiny piano. This grand piano probably costs more than his entire *house*.

Just wait until the clapping starts – *das gottverdammte Klatschen*.

He hates clapping. Hates hands. Beck's soul slumps and folds back into those tiny dark fantasies of having no hands, of not being physically *able* to do this. Wishes, just wishes.

He stays locked in them while the Maestro takes Joey off for *another* toilet break and more young pianists fill the room. At least they don't yap like the audience. Most are humming concertos under their breath, and their parents hover over them, more likely to puke with nerves than the performing kids. Everyone is under sixteen. In a few months Beck wouldn't even qualify for 'young' pianist. If the Maestro makes him enter adult contests? He'll crash and die. What is talented for a kid is average for an adult.

Beck closes his eyes. Forgets. Zones out so far he reaches the place deep inside where his own music lies. Little notes clamouring to be free. His own notes. His own creations. His fingers tap a tattoo against his other clammy palm.

If people cut him open, they'd never accuse him of being empty. He's not a shell of a pianist – he's a composer. Cut his chest and see his heart beat with a song all his own. *Oh look*, the world would say, *this boy is hiding a universe of wonder in him after all.*

'I said *hello*. Are you deaf or something?'

Beck's head snaps up so fast his neck twangs. When he loses himself like that it's hard to come back.

'Hi.' His voice is gravelly and he feels slightly dizzy. His fingers tap on his thigh, not the Chopin étude, but the music inside him.

'When do you play?'

Beck focuses on his interrogator. He probably should've stood up, shaken hands or – or basically done anything but sit like a surprised cod. She's nine, or ten, with hair like polished obsidian. She's the age where people still say 'Aw! Cute!' and then marvel at her ferocious playing. Beck lost the cute factor years ago. There's prize money and scholarships to be had today, and some little upstart like this will get them. There are ten contestants. They've been through scores of eliminations. They are the best ten the state has to offer.

'I'm last,' Beck says. The worst possible place. He'll lose all his nerve by then.

The kid's dress looks like a red cupcake iced with sprinkles. She folds her arms. 'How old are you?'

And he thought Joey had no manners. 'How old are you?' he shoots back, in control now.

'Ten. Erin Yukimura.'

'Fifteen,' Beck says. 'Kever—'

'I *know* who you are. Everyone knows the Keverichs.'

Beck stands and smooths his sweaty palms on his suit trousers. The suit is a little small, particularly around the wrists. He tugs the sleeves. How is he supposed to answer this kid?

How is he supposed to stand when the Maestro's piano has cast a shadow that stretches over half the universe?

Beck is saved by a boy in a shirt the colour of a blueberry. His smile is as wide as a watermelon slice and only adds to the fruity aura.

'I'm Schneider,' he says. 'I see you met the rabid Erin. Did she bite you?'

'Keverich,' Beck says and shakes hands with the blueberry.

'I know.'

It's unnerving. Beck would like to rip his last name into a hundred pieces and throw them into oblivion.

'Is she here?' the blueberry says. 'Your mother, I mean – Ida Magdalena Keverich.'

You don't address a famous retired pianist by half her name, of course.

'Is it true she only speaks German?' the rabid Erin says.

'She only swears in German.' Beck rocks on his heels. 'Actually, she only swears. What's the point of the rest of the language?'

'Does she still play?' The blueberry's eyes are so bright with longing that Beck looks away, disgusted.

'No,' he says.

Please, someone, drop the grand piano on Beck's head. It'd be a gift.

'If you played like her,' Erin says, 'I'd be terrified. But I've heard about you. And you're … not that good.' Her smile is a razor. 'I'll try to think of you when I win, but I probably will forget.' She smirks and skips off to her parents.

'There are some people,' the blueberry says, 'that you hope will slip off the stage and break both legs.'

'I feel you on a spiritual level,' Beck says.

The whispers of 'ten more minutes' tangle around the room and pianists start flexing fingers and taking a last sip of water. The co-ordinator checks in with everyone, makes sure they know when they'll be onstage for a seamless transition. By the time she gets to Beck, the blueberry farewells him with a handshake.

The Maestro sweeps back into the room. It's

her size, Beck tells himself, that commands attention. But her legacy as the most acclaimed pianist in Europe and sister to Germany's finest composer probably also has something to do with it. Also her hair. There's no way to tame the Keverich curls, and the Maestro looks like she's strolled through an electric field. Joey – in a puffy yellow dress and butterfly clips – has the same crisis going. And Beck? Even an entire tin of unfortunately expensive gel only gives the vague impression that his hair is slicked.

'*Bist du bereit?*' the Maestro says. *Are you ready?*

She's immune to the stares of the other parents and their tiny prodigies. This is the moment Beck should be proud his mother is famous. Instead he wants to climb on top of the piano and shout, 'IF ONLY YOU KNEW THE TRUTH.' She's a *monster*. Maybe once she was a dream of glory and excellence, but taking her talent took everything good.

Beck wipes his hands on his trousers again. '*Ja.*'

No

no

no.

Focus, Beck. Snap out of this. The music in his head crinkles and stops.

'You understand the importance of this contest,

mein Sohn?' The Maestro grips his elbow and pulls him to a quiet corner of the room. Her accent is thick. She's stressed. 'You will *not* let me down.'

'I won't,' Beck mutters. He feels smothered by stuffy backstage air, the deluge of hairspray to keep the Keverich curls controlled, the yards of material in the Maestro's gown from her glory days.

'Your time to prove yourself has ended,' the Maestro hisses. 'When you step on that stage, you represent me. I played these pieces when I was your age. Your uncle and I –' she makes a small noise of disgust, since she usually avoids talking about her brother, who is still famous and accomplished back in Europe and therefore annoying '– played these pieces until they became legacy. If your *schreckliches Spielen* disgraces me, I will not stand for it.' Her voice lowers, a deep growl. 'And there will be consequences. Do you understand me?'

Couldn't she say 'good luck, and remember to have fun!' and then promise ice cream no matter what?

Instead Beck imagines the slaps – or worse, something happening to Joey.

Why does she have to demand that he become her?

'*Ja*,' Beck says. *Thanks for the pep talk.*

The first pianist is shown on to the stage in a

wave of thundering applause. Then music – perfect music. Flawless with feeling and grace and the intricate detail of a lifetime of practice. Beck stands with the Maestro and the fidgeting Joey and tries to find his music again. His safe place.

The Maestro's fingers dig into his shoulder, her voice a knife in his ribs. 'Prove to me you are worth something.'

An 'or else' dances across Beck's vision. He flinches and says nothing, because nothing will convince her or please her or save him.

But the notes inside him roil and break and press so hard against his skin they'll rip the seams and he'll burst and – maybe they'll call him empty after all. Maybe no one can see his music, his *own* music, but him.

'I miss these days,' the Maestro says. 'I owned the stage and the music was mine. But look at me now.' Her shaking hands clench. 'You are a poor Keverich replacement.'

Beck shuts his eyes and waits until it's his turn to be executed.

CHAPTER 6

Last? Why did they make Beck go *last*?

Listening to the other pianists is excruciating. The blueberry plays unbelievably lightly, each note a clear ring of Mozart. There's no hesitation, no stumble. When the last notes have faded from the hall, the blueberry stands and bows and the applause is thunderous.

What if Beck fumbles the études, the Maestro's precious études? A cold shock of dread numbs his spine.

Every player, every piece, makes Beck feel like he's moving blindfolded towards a cliff. One slip and he's over.

The pieces are all under ten minutes, although

one girl pushes to the very last second with her Rachmaninoff concerto. Beck's playing two Chopin études, back to back, numbers eleven and twelve, and it should take him six and a half minutes.

Unless he passes out in the middle which, let's face it, is highly probable.

The rabid little Erin is directly before Beck – which is terror because she's wickedly good and melts the audience's hearts with her petite features and winning smile. Her hands dance an impossibly fast Liszt piece in B flat with a flawless finish. The audience are on their feet with applause.

When Erin struts off the stage like a sparkling cupcake of doom, she smirks in Beck's direction. 'Say bye-bye to the trophy, Keverich.'

Keverich.

It's the heaviest name in the world.

Every single thought flees Beck's head.

Everything is

fragments.

No, no, he can't be like this—

Pull yourself together, Schwachkopf.

They're ready for him to go on. The Maestro's fingers wrap around his arm, the only pressure keeping him from floating away. The world is a broken mirror, each shard reflecting his terrified face.

'*Do not fail,*' she hisses.

Beck's legs take him onstage. The silence pounds a symphony on his temples. The stage smells of wax floors and hot lights and shined leather. He tugs at his cuffs, wishes them longer, stops because he's being conspicuous. The lights are so bright the audience is reduced to unidentifiable black blobs.

Is that supposed to make them less daunting? Instead of eyes, he's watched by a sea of faceless ghouls.

He's at the piano. *Meine Güte*, it's huge.

The audience shifts, trying to remain patient after the hours of music, wanting to leave and hear the judges confirm their personal favourites as winners. Beck will be unmemorable – too gangly to be cute, too old to be incredible, too *stupid, stupid, stupid*. The piano is a beast and it owns him.

Stop cowering. He's done championships before. He's played in bigger halls.

This one shouldn't be different.

He slides on to the piano stool, still warm.

What if they picked him for last because he's a Keverich? *This kid will bring down the house*, they probably surmised, *if he's anything like his mother*.

But he's *not*. They've cut out his heart by making him last.

Beck's hands hover over the keys – rows of black and white teeth.

Play Chopin. Play fast and wild and *prove yourself.*

Just play the notes.

Notes.

Play.

Notes.

What – what – what is he meant to play?

Time knots around his throat. Hurry *up*. Think. He rakes desperately through his mind for the curls of notes he's practised all year, but the Chopin has gone.

There are no notes.

No. This *can't happen to him.*

Beck raises his head and sees the Maestro and the co-ordinator hovering at the edge of the curtains, petrified or furious, or both simultaneously. Stage fright doesn't happen with this level of competition. Shouldn't happen. They're better than this. He's better than this.

BUT HE HAS NO NOTES.

The Maestro won't stand for this – she'll think he's doing it on purpose.

Play something.

The Maestro will kill him.

Play something.

A wave sweeps over the audience, a murmur of confusion, a whisper of empathy at this poor darling trapped on stage with no notes. What a sad way to end an evening. They'll remember him for sure.

Play. Play. Oh – please – just – PLAY.

And he does.

At first Beck doesn't know what it is. They're notes, so that's a good start – but it's not Chopin's whispered opening and launch into a sharp rain of fast notes. This is dark and heavy, with bass chords that would make Rachmaninoff proud and an accompanying melody light as air. The music is sugar and charcoal. The bass crashes with something viciously violent in Beck's soul. So he repeats that part because it feels so good.

This piano will not make a fool of him. So he slams his fingers across the keys and owns it.

It's not Chopin.

Don't think about it now.

Beck's fingers calm and skate to the high registers, adding something sweet to the feast of darkness. It aches in minor, like butterflies and broken wings. If the audience doesn't lose some tears over this, they have no soul.

He leaves the butterflies bleeding over their wings and descends back to the pits of volcanoes and terror.

He plays like it's his last moment on earth. He plays so he feels like crying.

And then it's done.

Silence.

Sweat trickles down his forehead – sweat and tears and horror. They don't know if they can clap because this isn't a carefully metered classical piece they expected. It isn't on the programme. The judges – oh, the *judges*. He forgot he forgot he forgot—

He snaps to his feet, ready to bolt off the stage, but his legs are weak and it's all he can do to turn around and bow. That's when he realises they are clapping. It's not tentative or polite – it's bold and excited and amazed. There are flashes of colour and jewels and glints of teeth in smiling mouths as they stand. Every single person stands. Each clap says *what did we just hear*?

What did he just play?

The notes he's been doodling on his homework and tapping on his thigh all the way to the concert hall?

Beck finishes his stiff bow and walks off the stage. He left his lungs on the piano seat. He can't seem to breathe.

The applause fades as a microphone blasts to life – but Beck can't focus on words. Someone hands him a cold bottle of water and he slinks to a chair. Sits. Rolls the icy bottle over his forehead. His shirt sticks to his back and he feels hotter than the sun.

Where's the Maestro?

He blinks through a curtain of sweat and held-back tears and sees her. No eye contact. But Joey goggles at him.

He feels sick. Not nerves sick, fever sick, like he needs to cool down immediately or go supernova.

Backstage is a buzz around him, as notes are compared and the trophies are rolled out by stagehands. The co-ordinator flaps around trying to organise the kids so they'll be ready to walk onstage when called. Someone's parents are crying.

Then the microphone crackles and words smash into Beck's ears.

'... an unfortunate mistake which leads us to regretfully disqualify contestant number ten, Keverich, Be ...'

No.

He risks a glance at the Maestro. She's been carved from marble, every muscle taut and frozen.

The judge continues with, 'Though Keverich's performance was the most extraordinary thing I've encountered in thirty years of judging, it was not the required piece for this classical championship. Now, we move to the awarding of ...'

There are people talking to the Maestro. Her answers come slathered in a thick accent.

Beck zones out. He touches his own forehead and despite the galaxy exploding inside him, he's glacial cold. He feels dead. Bury him, please. What has he done? What has he *done*? He shuts his eyes against the burn of tears.

Cheers, clapping. Names. Trophies.

Did the blueberry place? Did – oh please no – did the rabid Erin take the trophy, the scholarship money, the promised lessons from a famous pianist?

Beck stares at his hands, his useless hands. He should've cut them off years ago instead of fantasising about it. Saved the world from hearing his agony made into music. Saved himself from the Maestro.

Something's definitely stuck in his eye.

The Maestro is in front of him, hauling him to his feet. She jerks his suit jacket straight, murmuring indecipherable German. They're leaving? Joey trots anxiously behind. They move through the maze of rooms and tunnels and down the stairs, out of an exit, and the cool night clasps Beck in its comforting arms.

He won't go to school tomorrow. He won't even move. He'll just fade into his bed and *he won't exist*.

It's late. The night has a wintry bite. The bus stop is nearly a kilometre of walking away, and their tickets are for midnight. Joey will want to be carried. Beck just needs to locate his feet, his wits, his strength, and get through this.

The walk is silent, brisk, with the Maestro holding Joey's hand so her small legs fairly run to keep up. No one can tell a dead boy walks with them.

What will she do?

They are a street away from the bus station and they pass the gate of a city park with huge heavy branched trees. Shadows hug their shoulders. The Maestro stops. She jerks free of Joey – who stumbles back, tired, surprised – and the Maestro turns on Beck.

He opens his mouth, but what's there to say?

She has height on him, strength, weight. Somewhere there is a man who is Beck's father and he must've been a skinny bean, because Beck sure didn't inherit his mother's physique.

She shoves him against the park gate with a clang. The air goes out of him.

Joey whimpers.

The Maestro has no words – not even a deluge of curses to outline his worth. She grabs him by the hair and slaps him. The sound of striking flesh is crisp, too loud, in the emptiness. Someone will see. Someone will stop her. Call the police, a mother hates her son.

The pain in his eyes must be encouragement, because she slaps him again.

Again – again – again.

Beck's lips splits, his mouth fills with blood, he's probably bitten his tongue in half. '*Mutter*, please,' he whispers. 'Not here.' A dribble of blood escapes his lips.

The Maestro must see the sense. She lowers her hand and releases Beck's hair so sharply he falls back and hits the gate again – this time with his skull. He grabs his head, spits blood, sinks to his knees. There's probably blood on his only good white shirt, so what'll he do next time? She'll be furious because of his shirt and it's not his fault. Not his fault.

The tears come in a blur, hot and heavy with hatred.

Joey is crying and whispering, 'Don't hurt Beck.' It comforts him, just a little.

'*Steh auf*,' the Maestro snaps. *Get up*. 'There is no word for what I think of you. You have destroyed me.'

Beck wipes his nose and smears wetness across his cheeks. Blood, snot? Does it even matter? He keeps his mouth closed, so nothing embarrassing can slip out.

The Maestro closes her hands into fists, but the shaking is ferociously visible.

'You are my disease,' she says, her voice eerily calm. 'You will kill me with your disgrace. But it will never happen again, will it?'

If he opens his mouth, an ocean will escape and he'll drown. He'll drown. Please don't make him answer.

She steps towards him, voice like a viper. '*Will* it?'

Beck's lips part and the last of his music slips free and dissolves in blood and tears.

'Never,' he says.

CHAPTER 7

Beck decides to rebel.

And by 'rebel' he means mostly lying in bed for two days straight, not making a peep, minding his manners, and cleaning the entire house for the Maestro, but still – *defiantly* – not playing the piano.

On the third day, he's still burrowed under the quilts when Joey invites herself in with breakfast in bed for him. She has one of her pink plastic toy trays with tiny pots of her infamous concoctions. He spies bread crusts on the tray and feels a stab of guilt. While he sulks, who takes proper care of Joey?

Her brow puckers, concentrating on not spilling

anything. 'I'm cheering you up since you're sick.'

Beck scoots into a sitting position as she lays the tray on his lap. Then she vaults on to the bed and nearly upends the whole thing in his face.

'Then we can go back to school.' She peers at him and squints. 'Do we have to wait until your face feels better?'

Beck picks up a teaspoon and prods one of the pots – is that uncooked rice and peanut butter? 'I don't know,' he says.

Any other parent would've hauled their teenage son out the door and lectured him about school. But Beck can skip three days and the Maestro won't say a word. In fact, the Maestro is ignoring him and thereby ignoring Joey. The message is loud and clear – her children are worthless brats.

And the Maestro won't walk Joey to school – as far as Beck knows, the Maestro hasn't left her room much either – but how long before someone asks questions about the absentee Keverich kids?

Beck cautiously eats sour yogurt sprinkled with flour.

Joey pokes his cheek. 'How much does it hurt?'

He glares. 'It hurts when you *touch* it!' The purple bruises cover his right cheek and his split lip has crusted in a scab. He just can't smile, really, which is fine by him.

Joey watches anxiously as he finishes the bread

crusts, which have been left plain to his relief. 'Is it good? Am I a good chef, Beck?'

'The best,' he says.

'Oh good.' Joey beams. 'I want you to feel all better. And I've got some extras –' Beck pales '– but if you don't want them, that's OK! I'll give it to August!'

Wait. What? 'August?'

'Yeah,' Joey says. 'She's outside. I told her we—'

Beck wrangles himself out of the sheets and shoots out of his bedroom. He lunges for the front window and cracks the blinds. Yes, she's there, swinging around a lamp pole, her lips puckered in a whistle. Has she been doing this every morning? Beck rakes his fingers through his hair and pulls hard.

Joey patters up behind him.

'You talked to her?' Beck says, strained. 'What did you tell her about me?' What if Joey splatters his embarrassing secrets? He'll never go to school again.

'I just said that your face was sad.' Joey sticks her lip out. 'And that you are a *meanie* because you haven't played with me for ever.'

'It's been three days.' Beck flies through the house and finds questionably clean jeans – screw the dress code – and a school shirt with holes in the collar. He slams a foot into his shoe so fast the tape snaps, and he has to spend precious minutes with string and scissors. 'Get ready, Jo!' he shouts. 'We're going.'

Joey barrels into her room screaming – probably from joy? Maybe? Who could know? She reappears with purple sparkly leggings, a jumper that says 'I Love The Brachiosaurus', her gumboots and swimming goggles.

No time to argue. He finds some old pizza buns in the fridge – if there's no mould, then they're OK, right? – and stuffs them into her lunch box.

As he's scooting them out of the door, he catches a glimpse of his face in the hall mirror. The swelling has gone down, but the handprint is pretty unmistakable. No one at school will care, of course – kids show up with broken arms and stitches all the time. Fights. Angry parents. Bike accidents. They live in that part of town. The school doesn't care if dozens of students have bruises or stitches or hollow eyes. It's too much and the teachers don't get paid enough for this.

But August will care.

Why does it matter?

Why is he even rushing to walk to school with her?

Because the last time they were together, he carried her home and he felt helpful and kind. And she thanked him. And it was *good*.

Beck locks the front door – he doesn't know or care where the Maestro is – and Joey sprints across the dewy grass to August.

'WE'RE GOING TO SCHOOL!' says Captain Obvious.

Beck suddenly remembers a million reasons why it's not OK to be around August. What is he doing? He feels like nine left elbows and a stomach full of butterflies. And his *face*.

But he deserved it. He failed. Just a simple task, play a Chopin piece, do it well, and he flunked it on purpose. Right? Did he even try? Did *he*?

He can't get rid of the pure elation of his own music flooding that hall. Or how thunderous the applause was. Or how beautiful it was, like a thousand stars exploding in his hands. It was even better than the rubbish he writes between classes.

But it was wrong – wrong – *wrong*.

August pops out two earbuds and stuffs her iPod in her pocket. She gives Joey a high five and then turns to – stare.

'Hi, Beck,' she says softly.

Beck wishes he could disappear or become someone else entirely.

He grabs Joey's hand and starts walking without a word, mostly because his brain is blank. He has no explanation why he wanted to see her. But now he's seen her and it's a mistake.

If August notices the ignored greeting, it doesn't show. She falls into step beside him, wearing tattered Converse on her feet for once, and bouncing a little with each step like there's music in her soles.

Is her foot OK now? Did her parents roast her for being violent at school? Did she really hang around his house waiting every morning? What does she want from him? What? *What?*

'So,' August says, dragging the word out to cover the galaxy of silence between them. 'You haven't been at school for a while.'

'I've been sick.' *Of everyone and everything.*

'What happened to your face?' Only a mouse could hear that whisper.

'I practised smiling,' Beck says. 'The mirror punched me for my efforts so, good news, you were right. I suck at it.'

He stares at the ground while he says this, counting the cracks, the times he steps over a broken bottle, how often Joey trips on the uneven cement.

'Oh, that's the thing about me,' August says, calm. 'I'm always right. You get used to it, especially if you practise saying "you were right, August! I was wrong" about fifty times before bed.'

'I'll remember.'

'Me too,' Joey says, squishing to walk between them.

They walk in silence, the weight of a joke and a lie as heavy as holding the world. Joey jumps cracks, yanking on Beck's arm at each leap, which only reminds him how much he aches.

It's only when Joey pauses to steal a handful of daisies from an unsuspecting garden, that August says, 'So what happened really?'

Joey sneezes into the flowers.

'I told you.' Beck knows the difference between caring and curiosity. Knowing someone for less than a week equals curiosity, *not* caring. 'And you know what they say in German.'

'Not really,' August says.

'*Halt die Klappe, du Schwein!*' Joey shrieks.

August blinks. 'Still not working for me.'

'Joey said to *shut up, you pig*,' Beck says. He shoves Joey into a puddle and she shrieks. 'But I was going to say: *das geht dich nichts an.*' He glances at her. 'Mind your own business.'

'I seriously don't know which of you is ruder at this point,' August says.

Joey points to Beck. 'He's grosser. Because he's a boy and boys are stinky.'

Beck swats at her but she runs ahead with a maniacal laugh.

August smirks.

What is with her? How come she refuses to get offended?

As if to prove how insults aren't going to deter her, August waits while he drops Joey at preschool and gets stampeded by a teacher wanting to know if she was sick, where the absentee note is, why she can't get hold of his mother by phone. Beck shrugs and mumbles and stumbles out to make a mad dash across the road as the last bell rings.

They fall into the tardy crowd as they make for the concrete stairwell to first period. A couple of guys are laughing way too loudly, and someone shoves into August and makes her trip up the last steps.

Beck could grab her arm, just to steady her.

He doesn't.

August clutches the rail and gives a fiery scowl. 'Get over yourself.'

A tall kid, with greenish blonde hair like he's been swimming in a pool of algae, sneers at her. 'Aw, sorry I tripped you. Did I hurt your feelings, tree hugger?'

August's face is pinched. Beck considers squeezing through the gap between her and Algae Hair and just going to class, but – but—

'I can give you a hug to make it up.' Algae Hair grabs for August's arm and she snaps away from him.

Beck does move through the gap between them, but he shoves Algae Hair hard on his way past. It gives August a second to get to the top of the stairs. But Algae Hair and his cluster of lowlifes are on their heels.

'What was that, then?' Algae Hair demands, lilting mockery gone. Because when a boy shoves a boy, it means blood and war, apparently.

Beck has no time for this. He rolls his eyes at August and pushes towards the hall.

Algae Hair gets in front of him. 'Did mummy give you a pat on the cheek?' he croons in a baby voice. 'Or is daddy too much of a pansy to use his fist?'

Anger ripples down Beck's spine. He's never been bothered by jerks, never even focused on them. And now? He wants to smash someone's living daylights out.

What's he becoming?

'Beck.'

He turns to August.

'This is, um,' she clears her throat, 'this is the butthead who I had a disagreement with last week. About the frog. I might've kicked him.'

'You didn't kick him hard enough.' Beck shoves past, his shoulder ramming into Algae's hard enough to emit a surprised grunt. Then, August beside him, they stride down the hall.

Algae Hair gives shouts at their backs, but they're all late. There are detentions to look forward to. A teacher is in the hall. It's not an auspicious day to be expelled.

They're about to separate, August to classes where people work, Beck to where they sleep – but she swings in front of him.

'I get that you won't do the paper,' she says, in a rush. 'So I'm just going to make up your part.'

'Or you could report me?'

'I might,' she says, 'or you'll tell me about your face and we'll call it even.'

Even? He'll get points for a paper he hasn't helped with?

'Or,' she says, 'I might just hang around *anyway*, until you tell me.'

'I'm not your friend.' It comes out jagged. 'My crap doesn't matter to—'

'I'll stick around,' she says fiercely.

Beck hesitates.

But he can't.

'I punched someone,' he says. 'They punched back. I'm actually a violent creep and you should go back to your real friends.'

August doesn't blink. 'You're a sucky liar. Guess I'm sticking around you.' She turns with a flip of her hair, and runs down the hall, only turning long enough to make a fist and point to her knuckles.

'Your hands. You didn't hit anyone.' Then she's gone.

Beck glances at his knuckles – not split or bruised. No. He never fights back, no matter how much he dreams about it.

He drifts into class and sinks into a desk like he's been there the whole time. No one notices. No one asks where he was the last few days or where the bruises came from. No one cares.

Why does August? There's something incredibly off about the way she bounces and how she insists on wearing colour – even if it is just some blue ribbon twisted around a lock of hair, or Sharpie scribbles on her arms. She's too happy for *real life*. That's it.

Life is rubbish. It's cruel and unfair and it always kicks the feet out from under you. It mangles dreams and spits in your face. When a kid turns fifteen, it's like understanding the bitterness isn't going to go away and life is destined to taste like sawdust. Fifteen is when kids get angry.

But August isn't.

It's not fair. His throat is hot and his eyes prick with crushing misery. It's not fair she gets to be happy.

CHAPTER 8

Beck sits by the football oval – far away from clusters of sociable teens – and regrets forgetting to grab a pizza roll for himself. August. She's to blame. She's a problem, any way he looks at it.

She's particularly a problem when she flops on the grass beside him with an apricot muesli bar, her satchel and an insufferable smile.

'I've tried to be nice about this,' Beck says, 'but I really can't stand your face.'

August peels her muesli wrapper. 'You break my heart. It's a pity I find your face so adorable. Well, the half that isn't purple.' She lies on her back and takes a bite of the muesli bar with a deep sigh.

Is she ... flirting?

'Don't you have friends?' Beck says. 'Or walls to kick?'

'I have friends.' August closes her eyes, like the muesli bar is such bliss. 'But what about you? How come I never see you chasing a footie with the other aggressive and hormonal boys who think grunting and kicking a ball is fun?'

'I'd rather stab myself in the face.'

August cracks an eye open. 'Aw. Somebody's had a bad experience with friends. Did no one share their toy cars with wittle baby Beck? Want to talk about it?'

'Hmm, let me see. No.'

August crooks her arm behind her head for a cushion and takes another bite of her muesli bar. 'You're so confusing, Keverich. One day you carry me home, the next you bite my head off. I used to have a dog like you. Completely psycho and always bit me and attacked anyone who even looked at it.'

'Let me guess. You cuddled it into submission?'

'Actually, Dad shot it.'

Beck chokes, like someone just punched his throat. He leans forward and hacks so violently, August has to pound his back.

'I'm joking!' She laughs.

'Ha,' Beck manages. 'Ha, ha.'

August shoves him lightly. 'My parents run a

veterinary and animal rescue. They're all about cuddling vicious dogs and feeding them treats.'

She finishes up the muesli bar and lets the crumbs drop to the grass. Beck hates how that bothers him. Such a waste. He'd give a lot to scoff a crumb by now, since dinner last night was nonexistent, breakfast a holy terror and lunch a blank slate.

'Are you going to feed me treats?' Beck inquires.

'If I thought it would work – absolutely.' August raises an eyebrow. She has ridiculously thick and wild eyebrows that quirk with every expression.

Beck gives a long-suffering sigh. 'Is there a reason you're still here?' At least he could drink to fill the black hole in his stomach. Water or water. Life is so full of fun options like that.

'Actually, yes.' August stuffs her wrapper back into her bag and rummages through the chaos of folders and papers. 'I've decided to contrast our music tastes for the paper.'

Music.

Why

would

she

choose

music?

Beck's mouth is dry. 'How is that political or moral?'

August has a sly look. 'And here I thought you weren't paying attention. But! Since you asked, it's religious. I'm going from the angle that some people worship musicians and bands get cult followings and I'll outline the difference between enjoying music and being obsessed with it.'

Sounds complicated. 'Well, great. I have a five-year-old sister who is addicted to bawling the Hokey Cokey all hours of the day. You can contrast that with – what do you listen to? They-kiss-they-break-up-they-kiss-again kind of stuff?'

August fishes a notebook from her bag, flips to a clean page – most of them are covered with doodles – and taps a purple pen against the spine. 'I listen to indie rock, actually. Ever heard of Lemon Craze or Twice Burgundy?'

'What kind of name is *Twice Burgundy*?'

'I don't know. *Once* Burgundy was taken? It has a nice ring to it. Tell me you've at least heard their song "Falling Into Technicolour"?'

They sound like idiots who compose lyrics out of weed and vodka. 'No.'

August slaps the notebook against her forehead. 'You're such a disappointment, Keverich.'

He ignores the knot in his throat.

'They're glorious.' August raises her arms like she's going to hug the sky. 'They're weird and most of their lyrics sound like they're high –' ha! He knew it! '– but they have *soul*, and I'm in love with one or both of them.'

Beck manages a strained smile. When will the bell ring and save him?

'So –' she's back to tapping the pen against the notebook '– names of your crappy rock bands that scream and howl?'

Wait while he just rolls out a list of Liszt, Grieg, Chopin and Bach. Wait while he explains how much better Steinway pianos sound over Yamahas. Wait while he explains that playing Rachmaninoff makes him feel powerful.

'Um, yeah.' Beck racks his brain for a name, *any name*. 'All of them really. So long as it's – um, loud.' If she presses for details, he'll just make a run for it.

August looks at him long and hard, then shrugs as if he's such a loser and scribbles notes. She's actually silent for a minute and Beck finds his fingers tapping a string of Chopin's notes absently. He stops and balls his hand into a fist. Can he explode from being such an idiot?

'You'll owe me, by the way.' August pauses and pokes the purple Sharpie dangerously close to Beck's nose. He lurches away. 'I haven't decided exactly, but it'll probably be you giving me chocolate every day for a month.'

'I'm pretty sure "no" is the only way to answer that.'

Maybe he *would* buy her chocolate as a thank you – if he had money. But if he had money he'd buy Joey an ice cream or get himself some jeans that aren't too short.

'Or,' August says, 'you agree to a friendship truce.'

'But "friendship" implies we're friends –' *and we're not* '– and "truce" implies we're fighting.'

'We aren't fighting?'

'I would call it "stiff acquaintance with a touch of hate".'

'I'm not stiff.' She flings an arm around his neck. 'And I don't hate you.'

Beck peels away. 'You will. Give it time.'

'Then cut class with me.'

Beck stares.

'Oh, don't act righteous.' She pulls a hairband from her wrist and knots her hair into a thick bun. 'You showed up to school, so that's half the battle, and I think you and your purple face could use a morale boost. I could use a mental health day.' She stuffs her notebook back into the satchel. 'We'll go on a quest to find cake.'

She bounces to her feet and stretches a hand to him.

Beck Keverich doesn't act. He fantasises. He longs. But he does exactly *what he's supposed to do.*

Until he takes her hand and she yanks him upright and he somehow says, 'It better be a big cake,' and they abandon education and sneers and presumptions that he's a punch bag and she's a tree hugger, and they escape to be different people entirely.

It should be an impossible task. Finding cake? Leaving school grounds? Wearing a uniform? Beck is entirely certain someone will point and shout 'THEY'VE ESCAPED THEIR PRISON!' and haul them back.

Either August doesn't share this fear or doesn't think it's impossible.

August probably exists in an alternate reality where nothing is impossible and no one is too mean and the sun doesn't stop shining.

They cut across the football oval and battle their way through a small patch of scrub to the road. From there it's a stroll to a nearby shopping complex. It's nothing fancy. Most of the shops have bars on the windows and the ones with the most business are cheap one-dollar shops and McDonald's. It's excruciating bypassing the smell of hot chips and cheesy burgers. He'd eat just about anything by this point.

But August leads him to a coffee shop in a poky corner that has exactly zero customers but them.

None of the tables and chairs match, and

daffodils sit in beer bottles as centrepieces. One wall is a chalkboard with a million scribbles in every colour and the other is crammed with mismatched photo frames. Dreamcatchers hang across the entrance so thickly, one smacks Beck in the face – and then swings around to smack him in the back of the head as well.

'What exactly do they sell here?' Beck rubs his skull and stares at a pile of bongo drums, which might be for decoration or for spontaneous costumers to thump.

August wags her finger at him. 'When a person buys you cake, don't question anything.'

'Can I question the cake's ingredients?'

'No, you ungrateful whelp. You eat it, even if it's made of chia seeds.'

What – what are *chia seeds*? Are they even a real thing? Is this his last meal on earth—

'Beck,' August says patiently, 'this is an alternative café. Just sit down and keep your mind open.' She points to a table that is probably an antique and a chair that is probably from the dump. 'And please don't make horrified noises.'

'Alternative as in *how*?' Beck's voice is pitched a little high. 'They sweeten the cake with human hearts?'

'Um, more like alternative-as-in-the-cake-is-sweetened-with-stevia.'

Beck sits down. 'Is the death short and easy?'

August swats him.

She slips around the register – Beck is pretty sure that's not how you order – and disappears through a curtain of beads to the kitchen. There are distant pots clanging and panpipes droning from a single dilapidated speaker. August is only gone a heartbeat before shouts and greetings explode from the kitchen and someone bawls August's name like they haven't seen her in nine years.

Beck wants to regret coming – it's just too *weird* – but he's so hungry.

August reappears, clearly pleased with herself. 'My mum's best friend's cousin works here. Everything is half price for me. Also he won't tell the school or my parents.'

'Aren't we lucky.' Beck's voice is dull. 'I have to get my sister at three.'

'We have time.' August's ocean eyes settle on Beck's face with a serious and piercing look that makes him uncomfortable. 'I'm almost entirely certain it'd take you less than ten seconds to demolish a cake, anyway. Do you ever eat?'

'I eat,' Beck says, defensive.

'My dad would take one look at you and try to fatten you up.' August shakes her head, smiling.

It's strange to Beck how she mentions her parents offhandedly, lovingly, like they don't rake

94

her over the coals on a regular basis or spit out how much they loathe her.

'You'll meet them when you come over,' she says.

'What?'

'Oh, you will eventually. I know these things.'

Beck resists the urge to catapult out the door. Why does August make him want to run *and* stay at the same time? How come he can't muster the energy to truly get rid of her? Because she pays attention to him? Because she laughs instead of seethes at his snarky quips? Because she's buying him cake?

The last one. It's the last one.

A server swishes out of the beaded curtain carrying a tray that looks like it was made from an old crate. He has long dark hair that hangs to his shoulders and tie-dye fisherman pants that balloon so much they look like a skirt. But his shirt says *Hate On Me And I'll Punch You*, which kind of throws the chill vibe.

Beck wisely decides not to hate on him. Ever.

'Yum, thanks, Morris,' August says. 'It looks delicious.'

A violent hippy named *Morris*?

'Anything for our favourite August.' Morris sets plates and mugs down and smiles crookedly. 'Not going to snitch, but skipping school ...' He tuts. 'Dude.'

'I know, I know.' August turns into a pathetically adorable puppy dog. 'But just look at my friend – he's practically starving to death.'

Morris squints at Beck. 'Well, he looks your type, I guess.'

'Um,' says Beck.

'You know,' Morris says, 'pitiful and starved.'

'Thank you, Morris,' August says. 'Goodbye, Morris.'

'All right, all right.' He shrugs, tucks the tray under his arm and ambles back to the kitchen.

'How many pitiful and starved boys do you bring here?' Beck says, slightly strangled.

August spins her plate as if the cake will taste better from a specific angle. 'Shut up and eat, Keverich.'

Beck pokes the cake with his fork. It doesn't look indigestible – but he is used to Joey's cooking – and it appears to be stuffed with nuts and dried fruit. The drink has a thick creamy froth with cinnamon dusted on top. It smells like ... *not* chocolate or coffee. What is it supposed to be?

What has he gotten into?

August has already tucked into her cake with a few moans of deliciousness.

'So,' he says, forking up cake and staring at it, 'am I eating Steve?'

'It's *stevia*.' August licks her fork. 'An alternative

for sugar. But don't say *that* S word here.'

Beck's too hungry. He stuffs the cake in and mumbles, 'Is there a swear jar in case I need to say – holy *shit*, what is this amazingness?'

August tips back her head and laughs.

Beck abandons the fork and just picks up the cake and takes a mouthful. It's like fruitcake but also *almonds* and also *small explosions of chocolate* and the occasional chewy date. He's never tasted anything so good and dense.

'I could eat, like, nine pieces,' he says with his mouth full.

'I knew you'd like it.'

'Actually –' Beck licks his thumb '– you totally doubted.'

'Fine. I did. But I was going to punch you in the face if you didn't.'

'Really? So you secretly wanted me to hate it so you could live that dream.'

August puts her elbows on the table and points her spoon at him. 'You have such bad self esteem, it's kind of sad but still adorable. The truth is, I tried to bring my *friends* here and they ...' She sits back in her chair, face clouded. 'They were pretty rude about it all.'

'That sucks.' Beck only has half his mind on the fact that August maybe doesn't fit with her friends like he always thought, and half on the fact his cake is gone. 'I would never be rude, of course.'

August snorts, but she slips from her chair and disappears back into the kitchen. She returns with another slab of almond fruitcake, bigger than before.

Beck remembers to thank her, but then he has to concentrate because a clump of chocolate has melted in the centre and he needs it *all* in his mouth. Right now. This is so much better than a bite of fluffy sponge cake. This cake glues to his ribs.

The drink – a dandelion latte, August explains – isn't as delicious, but he still drinks the entire thing and probably would've taken a refill. Or ten. Maybe he did like it? Maybe he likes everything. Maybe *this* is why August is so happy. Cake! And coffee – well, um, whatever-it-was! On a regular basis!

'It could be a little sweeter, though, don't you think?' Beck says – at the wrong time, since Morris walks out of the kitchen to wipe another table.

The stiff look says he offended Morris.

'I'm sorry,' Beck whispers to August. 'It's just the tea had that something-is-dead-in-here vibe, you know?'

August punches him. 'You're uncultured. But we'll build up slow. Today almond cake, tomorrow turmeric broth and alfalfa patties.'

'I'd very much like to leave now.'

August disappears to pay and appease the hurt Morris, and returns with a paper bag of biscotti. She shakes it in Beck's face. 'For Joey. Now for a leisurely stroll back.'

Beck is horrified. He totally *forgot* about Joey. What kind of a horrible brother is he? This dampens his elation over a full stomach down and he settles into an easy walk beside August. He's not sure what to think of their outing. Not sure what to think of her.

And maybe he should shut up, accept the cake and the olive branch, accept the insistent kindness. But, as they exit the shopping complex, bypass piles of stolen trolleys in a ditch and stumble on the cracked footpath, he has to ask.

'Why are you really doing this?' Beck says quietly.

Please, universe, don't let her say *because you're pathetic and need a friend* or *you're clearly starved and abused so I'm doing my duty*. Although what's left for her to say?

August doesn't answer right away, which is good – she's thinking seriously for once.

'You're interesting, Beck Keverich, even though you won't tell me your full name or who hit you.' She walks on the edge of the gutter, arms out for balance, bag of biscotti crinkling in the wind. 'You're kind, but you're also mean – and that's confusing. You get super crabby when you're hungry.' She flashes a cheeky grin. 'But I fixed that for now.'

He considers shoving her into a puddle.

August sobers. 'You're like this overlooked shadow, always in the background, and you make me so *curious*. And your life obviously isn't all peach pie and daffodils and I figure that equals a body needing a friend. You're weird. I'm weird. Why not? Oh.' She pauses. 'Nearly forgot. You have freaking beautiful eyes.'

His throat knots.

August jumps off the gutter and turns to face him. 'I don't have to know. I won't keep asking. But you know where I live, so if you want a break from –' she waves vaguely at his face '– *it*, you can come over. Any time.'

Self-conscious, Beck touches his scabbed lip, his swollen cheek, and drowns in the suffocating knowledge that someone notices.

And cares.

CHAPTER 9

The Maestro doesn't end his unprecedented holiday.

Beck does.

For habit? To please her? Because, even though it hurts, he's addicted?

Beck plays scales to unravel the stiffness in his fingers, to shake off the week he spent in silence. Then he tackles exercises that go faster and faster like a thousand marbles falling down the stairs. But the pieces? The Bach, the Schumann, the Chopin – every time he tries to play them, the notes blur and he has to scrub knuckles over his scalp in nervous agony. Because he sees –

the thrum of the audience,

the molten fury on the Maestro's face,
the stagnant silence while he gropes for music,
the failure, strangling him.

Even after an hour of irritatingly repetitive scales, his fingers ache for his own music instead of the Maestro's. But he doesn't dare let his notes breathe.

He plays for hours. He forgets cake and freedom and August. It's better this way.

He plays until eight and only stops because he hears Joey readying for bed. She shouldn't have to listen to him pound out B flat scales while she sleeps. Instead, he searches for food – which proves harder than spotting a platypus. It looks like the Maestro had tinned spaghetti, so Beck heats a plastic bowl for himself and scribbles music on the back of an old docket while he eats.

Only the click of spoon against bowl tells the house he's alive. He's *there*.

So he daydreams about music – *his* music – and what it'd be like to have it written out. He mentally adds in a few strings, some brass, and wonders if he could juggle a whole orchestra in his head.

He wonders if he'd make the Keverich name proud by composing instead of playing.

As if the Maestro would let him. Ha.

There is his uncle, famous pianist and composer, but the fact that the Maestro curses and praises him all in one breath – because he can still play music and she can't? – cements the fact that the Maestro would be furious if Beck started composing. Besides, she never composed, so why would he need to when she demands he follow in her footsteps? Beck can't even play the études that the Maestro and her brother had perfected with their eyes closed at his age. How dare he write his own music? If he even whispered about dreams of composing, she'd see it as rebellion and descend into a rage.

She strides into the kitchen then, the room shrinking around her as she fills it with her scowl, her height, her expectations. They haven't spoken since the contest, haven't even looked at each other. Beck's toyed with the idea she might give up on him completely and just *ignore* him – which would be, basically, the best thing ever.

Without a word, she slaps the kettle on and digs for a mug and a teabag.

And he hates her for it.

The Maestro doesn't act like one who's been broken in half. She doesn't cower in a crippled heap or huddle in tearful *what if*s.

But Beck does. And he has the use of *both his freaking hands*.

It makes him want to hurl his lukewarm spaghetti, to stand, scream, *rage* at how he's treated when he didn't ask for this, when he didn't cause the end of her career. The stroke did.

Beck touches his once-split lip. Remembers.

The Maestro's spoon tinkles against the mug as she pours hot water. 'Have you finished practising?'

Is that a trick question? Beck spins his empty bowl. 'Well, Joey's in bed, so – I don't want to disturb her.' Not a yes or a no. Nicely done.

'I have not heard the études yet.' She reaches for her mug handle but stops, her hand shaking too hard. She rests it on the bench and still doesn't look at her son.

As if he's forgotten the doomed études. But what can he say? *Um, no, because I'm not planning to touch them ever again?* He'd rather pretend those études never existed, that he'd never sat on that stage and forgotten them.

She picks up her mug and takes a sip. '*Geh,*' she says. 'Go.'

'But, it's so late …' Beck trails off.

Her eyes are flints of steel.

He abandons his red-stained bowl in the sink and marches to his piano, because, apparently, she will not let this one go. The reprieve was a joke.

The Maestro follows him. She sets her mug on some old music on top of the piano – Beck notices the red marks on her hand, fresh burns from where she's spilt hot tea and is too proud to bandage. She nods for him to start.

Beck pulls out the music, slightly crumpled, from the piano seat. But as soon as he smooths it out, the Maestro snatches it away and tosses it on his bed.

'By memory.' She stabs a finger at his skull. 'You know them. You *know*.'

'I forgot.'

Her fingers curl into a fist, but the blow doesn't land.

Beck flinches. 'I *have* forgotten,' he whispers. 'I swear, I – I don't know what happened, I—'

'Play!' she barks.

Beck rests his hands on the keys, shifts around a little and frantically tries to remember the notes. But they're *gone*. They're gone – gone – gone—

She slams her forefinger on the first note, the *right* note. And it hits him in a rush. Yes. That's the chord. His fingers find it and press.

The Maestro's eyes are hot on his neck. 'You do not forget music, *Junge*. It is always in your head.' She takes the opportunity to stab him with her finger again. 'But what are you doing? *Stopp!* Are you a timid lamb?' Her voice rises.

Beck retracts his hands from the keys.

She cuffs the back of his head and he lays his hands back on them.

'Do you play the notes like they'll bite you,

Junge? Or do you play with fire, with passion, like they're the only important notes in the world? These études are my legacy – will you spit on that?'

The look in her eyes says she'd like nothing more than to sweep on to the piano herself and play and play and *never ever stop*. But she hasn't touched the piano since her hands started shaking. Beck wonders how much she misses it – the lights, the stage, the applause, the people recognising the true talent of a musician whose soul is woven with the piano. Was she happy back then? Was her life thousands of notes knitted with smiles and congratulatory roses clasped in her perfectly poised hands?

She picked his entire repertoire out of pieces she excelled at. Pieces that made her famous, that she swears will make *him* famous. She knows them better than her own heartbeat. Which is why she hates when he butchers them. He wishes he didn't. He wishes, just once, he could play them perfectly for her since she's had every note she loved snatched away.

'I swear I just forgot,' Beck says. 'Please, I'll relearn it. I just need the music—'

The smack is harder this time and his neck snaps forward, nearly whacking against the piano.

Her voice is calm now, calm but bitter. 'Why do I wish you to play the piano?'

Another trick question. Beck opens his mouth,

but the words have sped away. *Because you want to control me? Because you failed so I have to succeed?*

Beck stares intently at the keys.

The Maestro gives him a shove and somehow, defying physics and the tiny constraints of his room, she slides on to the piano stool next to him. She doesn't hit him. She sits, rigid and austere, and Beck loses all sense of what's normal, what's right, what's expected. He can barely breathe.

'There is music inside you,' the Maestro says. 'Just as there was inside of me.'

It's not what he expected.

'My music was taken,' the Maestro says, stoic, though Beck can see, out of the corner of his eye, how her hands are shaking. 'You still have yours. Do you squander the gift? Do you ignore it?'

'I don't,' he says, not sure if he's defending himself or making a promise.

She curls her fingers into a fist to stop the trembles. 'It means nothing to you, when it should mean everything.'

It shouldn't hurt, not after everything, but his eyes feel hot and he wishes she'd just shut up and go away. She's told him all this, a hundred times.

How hard would it be to say *good job, you can do better because I believe in you*?

'I want the best for you, *Sohn*,' the Maestro says.

Please. She wants what's best for *herself*.

The Maestro continues, 'I want your music, I want *you,* to mean something in this world. Your uncle comes on tour to our country soon and you will play for him. Amazingly. You *will*.'

It's *nearly* a nice pep talk. But his uncle? More mountainous expectations for him to fail? Great.

'Play,' she commands. 'Play the Chopin. Play it right.'

So he does.

It comes back, with hesitating mistakes at first, and then he remembers. The chords wrap around his fingers as he kneads them out of the piano. He tries to play softly, because of Joey, but the Maestro raps her knuckles on his head, so he throws himself into the music.

Music is nothing unless it fills your soul with colour and passion and dreams.

But Beck can't find it, *can't* stitch that passion into this music that isn't his own. He can hit every note right, but what's the point? She'll never say *well done*. She'll never smile after he masters a difficult run. He plays like a boy trying too hard, with fingers that are tired to the bone.

Somehow he still wants her face to break into a smile, like it did when he was little, and her chin to tilt back with a tidal wave of laughter as she proclaims her son a prodigy.

Instead he plays the études.
Over and
over.
And over
once more.

The Maestro stands, nods, her foot taps to the music. 'Play it every day, every single day, until you *cannot* forget it.'

'Yes, *Mutter*,' Beck says, beaten.

Is this punishment for having a friend? For finally *doing* something instead of *wishing*?

These eighty-eight keys are part of him, but do they have to be his whole life?

His jaw tightens until he thinks it'll break off – and his fingers crash the étude finale. He looks at her, fiery and defiant for half a second, daring her to point out the wrong notes. Daring her to say he's worthless.

The Maestro's eyes are sad or wistful – or dead. He can't tell. 'You could be something, *Schwachkopf*. You could be.'

But he's not, is he?

Is

he?

She leaves without saying he played badly.

CHAPTER 10

There's no torture like a song on repeat.

Beck can't shake the étude, can't shake the weariness after playing half the night, can't shake the feeling that the Maestro has been different – weird – since she said he *could be something*. He doesn't know what it means.

Does it mean anything?

Ugh, he's tired.

But, congratulations to the universe, the Chopin is burned in his brain so fiercely that he wishes he could slam his head against a wall to quiet it.

Instead, he goes to school.

It's been weeks since the cake escapade, but Beck still gets a pang when he sees August – what is it? Nerves? Anticipation? He knots up, hunches his shoulders and can't think of anything to say. Until she gets talking. Until he defrosts. Until they find their pocket of comfortableness to stroll in.

It's wet and cold when Beck and Joey exit the house for school. Joey wears a bright red raincoat and basically looks like a hazard sign. Beck has an oversized hoodie, but it's hardly waterproof. And August, as usual, is entirely underdressed. She has on shoes, at least, with knee-high neon striped socks, but no jumper. Her flesh is a ripple of goosebumps as they walk in the misting rain.

'I'm gonna jump in puddles!' Joey warns and then dashes a few paces ahead.

'You'll get wet—' Beck says, but Joey just swears at him in German and pounds the footpath. Oh, forget it. The preschool teacher can figure out what to do with a soaked five-year-old.

'I finished the paper.' August pats her satchel. 'It's downright inspired.'

'What if they know I did nothing?'

'You'll get detention. Or expelled. And you kind of deserve both, but –' she wiggles her eyebrows '– I am, fortunately, super nice. I wrote your section with my left hand so it looks crappy enough to pass for you.'

'You are nice.'

'"You" –' August wraps it in air quotes '– are a

horrific writer compared to my eloquent soliloquy. But I had to make myself look good. No offence.'

Beck shrugs.

'You say a few dumb things,' August adds. 'But I'm not here to make you look intelligent. I'm not a miracle worker.'

'I can live with that.'

'You do have a fanboy moment.' Her grin is evil. 'It's hilarious. You misuse the word incredulous, but your gist is that you *adore* this hardcore rock band. Who'd have thought quiet ol' Beck could be so passionate about music?'

Ha. The irony.

August pauses to wrestle with her satchel and yank out her iPod. She peels wet hair off her face and tucks an earbud in, hands covering the iPod screen to protect it from the worst of the mist. Is this the end of the conversation? Beck isn't sure if that's a relief or a disappointment.

But August yanks the bud from her ear and shoves it at Beck. 'Listen to this. You *have* to. Your existence depends on it.'

'Meaning what? You're going to kill me and toss me in some ditch if I don't?'

'Yes,' says August sincerely. 'Don't turn me into a murderer. Just listen to it.'

Beck takes the extended iPod gingerly, like it's going to combust. The last thing he feels like is listening to music. He craves silence.

'Um, you do know how to work an iPod, right?' August says.

Beck realises he needs to do more than put the earbuds in. He jabs the play button and gives her a withering look – even though he, truly, has no idea how to work an iPod.

She raises her hands in protest. 'I've never seen you within ten feet of a computer! Or with a phone. Or even a calculator.'

'So you assume I'm rubbish at technology?'

August rolls her eyes. 'Focus on the song, Keverich. Embrace your Twice Burgundy education.'

But they're at an intersection, which means pausing and taking one of Joey's hands each and swinging her as they cross. Then Beck's left with August's favourite band in his ears.

Sharing music is personal because music speaks, it feels, it breathes. And it always says something about you.

Beck listens.

What did he expect? Drunk lyrics and panpipes? Instead there's an acoustic guitar and voices blended in aching perfection. One minute they are fast and violent as a summer storm – and then they're sharing a lullaby of bittersweet change and loss.

He's never heard music like this before.

It's not like he's a contemporary music virgin. He's listened to – stuff. Ads on TV for one thing. Shopping centre speakers blasting the latest chart-topping single. The neighbours playing a thumping bass tune for twenty-four hours straight to get back at Beck's midnight piano practices. There used to be yelling matches over the fence about this, but you don't win arguments with the Maestro. They eventually gave up and ignored their bruised, incessant piano-playing neighbours.

But August's music tastes different. He wants more.

It's been three songs and he hasn't said a word and suddenly they're at the preschool gate. Disorientated, he jerks the buds out of his ears and rushes Joey into school. Then he's out, clutching the iPod, feeling breathless like he just woke up and realised his dispassionately grey existence is actually tinged with colour.

August's lips twist in a smirk. It's annoying, but he's lost for words. His brain throbs entirely with music.

'You like them,' August says. 'You *adore* them. You realise you haven't been living without Twice Burgundy in your life.'

'Are you kidding? I hate it.' Beck wonders how he can get more of this. He needs more of it.

August snorts. 'Of course you hate it. If you

114

want, you can borrow my iPod for the day and continue hating it.' With a flip of her hair and the hip-length necklaces she's wearing this morning, August stalks off. 'Don't get it confiscated!' She's swallowed by a huddle of friends – odd friends with mismatched shoes or crutches or twitches, who hug her hello and lean close to share a story. Is August just magnetised to the broken misfits?

Beck holds the iPod like it's his entire life and he wonders why his stupid feet don't run after her and say something simple, something nice, like:

Thanks, August, these songs saved my life.

Beck decides to hide and avoid August – for the entire day. For someone who's absconded with her iPod, it's rude, but he wants to listen. Needs to listen. He loves the way her music drowns the études in his head. But he hates the way he craves it.

It's really August's fault, because she has thirty-six Twice Burgundy songs and he has to hear them all.

Beck hides out in the library over lunch – the absolute *last* place anyone would guess. He squishes between the rows of non-fiction and eats a tinned beans and jam sandwich, stuck together with toothpicks that nearly impale his throat. Thanks, Joey.

He even gets away with earbuds in class since the rain has sent everyone mental. Half the kids come in from lunch coated in mud from a footie game. Everything smells stale and wet. The teachers flap between giving suspensions and mopping mud and instructing that-kid-who-fell-in-a-puddle to stand below the heater – which turns out to be set on cooling and probably gives the kid hypothermia.

Beck watches dispassionately and inhales music.

August catches up with him at the preschool gate, when he emerges with Joey, a note to the Maestro about Joey's worryingly violent behaviour in class, and a spaceship made from yogurt containers and painted hot pink.

'If you carry it for me, I'll love you for nearly ever,' Joey says passionately.

'Uh-huh.' Beck hoists it up, one earbud still in.

She kisses his elbow and prattles on about her creation.

Some kids on the bus jeer as they exit the preschool with the pink catastrophe. He doesn't care, but he wishes he could cover Joey's ears.

August looks like a bedraggled bird. She's taken her neon socks off and slipped them over her arms, which is probably warmer but terrible to look at.

'Are you going to skip town with my iPod?' Her eyes sparkle like his avoiding her is actually the most amusing thing of the day.

Beck hands it back, struggling with the spaceship. Joey trots behind him, clutching her hands together in anxious worry that he might drop it.

'I forgot I had it,' Beck says. 'Just sat in my backpack all day.'

'You were listening just now.'

'Hm? What? No, I wasn't.'

She gives him a playful shove and he has to leap over a puddle, clutching the spaceship as if his life depends on it. It does. An elbow-kiss can quickly turn into a shin-kick when it comes to Joey.

'Be careful!' Joey screeches and leaps over the puddle after him. Except she misses and ends up in the middle. She wades out scowling. 'No pushing, August, or I'll—'

August raises her hands. 'Sorry! Sorry! I didn't think. But Beck has incredible balance, don't you, Beck?'

'Absolutely.' He tries to turn the spaceship around so Joey doesn't see it's totally dented on one side.

They resume walking, more docile now. But August is practically glowing with *I told you so*.

'Which song is your favourite?' she says. '"The Agony of Two Freed Souls in a Green Land"? Or "Morning in the Lonely Space"?'

'That one called "Grill"?'

August smacks her hand against her thigh. 'Oh,

yes. "Grill". I love "Grill". I love how it doesn't even fit with the other songs, but it's still *amazing*.'

Beck wants to scoff, but he can't. If he let himself, if he slipped up for just two seconds, he could fall in love with that music and talk about it for years.

'It's inspired,' August says. 'Twice Burgundy fling us into space and stars and galaxies and show us how to breathe.'

He shrugs. 'They're OK.'

Her glare is nearly formidable. 'Stop it, Keverich. Stop *pretending*. You ran off with my iPod, which means you're about to marry all the Burgundies like I am.'

Joey, elbows out, shoves between them. 'Who's marrying a burger? I want to marry a burger.'

'I want to marry a burger too, Jo,' Beck says. 'But right now, August and I are talking about – a harem?'

'Polygamy. Shared custody of our true loves,' August says. 'Because Beck finally understands what *real* music is. Not your heavy clashing rock stuff.'

Wouldn't it be nice to tell her? Right now? To just open his mouth and let it tumble out – about the music in his head that burns to be played, how the Chopin études are ruining his life, how the Maestro hates him because he's not good enough.

How he's suffocating between piano keys.

But he says, 'My music is awesome, thank you very much,' and a little bit of him dies.

'What?' August tilts her head. 'I can't hear you over the sound of my music being *abso-freaking-lutely* better than yours.'

They're in sight of the house now and Joey dashes ahead to open the door so Beck can get her precious creation inside.

Beck pauses to check the mail – or is he just delaying the goodbye to August?

'You don't listen to a lot of music, do you?' she says.

'Not this kind,' Beck says.

'Well, I'm glad I could introduce you to paradise.' August gives him a salute with her sock-covered arms. 'But careful, Beck. You've started acting like a nice person.' She turns and runs down the wet road, her hyena laugh flying behind her.

Beck knows. He should do something about it. *Should ...*

... but.

He follows Joey inside, peels off wet shoes and socks and gently sets Joey's creation in the kitchen. Then he disappears while she shrieks at him in German because of the dint.

He's nearly smiling, nearly *happy* – or something – until the Maestro appears in his doorway.

He's got a clean, dry shirt half over his head and a sudden sick feeling in his stomach.

The Maestro holds a stack of graded theory sheets. Is it just Beck or has the red pen grown wilder, the handwriting more unreadable? Maybe her hand tremors are getting worse.

'Remember how I said *mein Bruder* is coming out from *Deutschland*? It's happening now. Arrangements are being finalised for his tour next month.'

Ah, his uncle-she-curses-because-he's-still-a-successful-pianist-and-she's-not.

Beck tugs the collar of his polo shirt. Is he supposed to say something here?

'He's agreed to hear you.'

Oh.

'But – but that doesn't, I mean – what does it mean?' Beck says.

'It means *everything*,' she snaps, like he's being ungrateful.

He's not allowed to be confused? *She's* throwing the bombshells.

'If you impress him, he'll give you lessons to correct your sloppy technique.'

'Like, one lesson?' Beck says and hesitates. 'Because then he's going back to Germany?'

The Maestro's lips thin. 'Unless a miracle happens and he is impressed by your playing.' Her eyes say that's unlikely. 'If so, you can return to Germany with him and work hard and make the Keverich name proud.'

Wait.

Did she –

she didn't.

'Mum,' he says, forgetting German, forgetting to paint his voice with respect. 'Mum, I'm fifteen. I'm not even finished with school. You can't just toss me into another country. I—'

'If your uncle takes you,' the Maestro says, 'you go.' Like that's the end of it. Like nothing else matters.

'What if I mess up again?' It's out before he thinks. Why is he always so *stupid*? He says it like a challenge, like a threat, and his face is hot with preparation to be slapped.

What if I purposefully mess up?

What if I refuse?

'That is why,' the Maestro says, 'you will practise the études without fail. That is why you will work *hard*. Jan Keverich is the leading pianist on this earth, this *earth*. To have him accept you as a pupil would mean—' She stops, flushed, excited, out of control. 'A future. The Keverich line of fame will not die.'

He holds back tears.

The Maestro clears her throat, her arms tight

around the red-inked theory pages. 'It would mean you *are* something. Don't you want that?'

Yes – but. No?

It could be an escape, for ever. He could leave behind this hellish room, the tongue lashings, the hateful glances, the reminders of how much he's *failed her*. He could stop looking at her ruined, shaking hands with that mixture of relief and guilt.

He could be free.

'Practise.' The Maestro sweeps out of his room.

On the other side of the house, Joey yells for Beck to come and fix her spaceship.

If he was gone, the Maestro would start on Joey.

The piano glints a toothy smile.

So Beck sits down, and plays, and plays and *plays* – his own music – with breathless passion.

He won't go.

CHAPTER 11

August (and sort of Beck?) gets an A on the paper.

Beck's never scored so high. In fact, it's so unlike him Mr Boyne requests August and Beck stay behind to be scrutinised. August, with an innocently angelic smile, swears they did it together.

Beck's not sure if he should admire her ability to convince people so easily or be terrified.

On the walk home, August demands celebration.

'It's not like *you* did anything,' she says, 'but I need congratulating. Tomorrow's Saturday. What about that park we always cut through? We could meet up there at four and Joey can play. I'll bring cupcakes.'

Beck has a small panic attack. 'I can't—'

'Refusal is not an option.' August takes off for her own house, yelling over her shoulder, 'You owe me!'

He *does*.

But what are they going to do at that playground? Hang out? He's sure that's where the drug dealers make their drops.

How does he ask permission?

If the Maestro is home in the afternoon …

But she's not. At midday, she leaves for the bus to do some jobs in town – probably eating out too, since there's no food in the house and she never seems to go hungry like he and Joey have to. She commands Beck to practise hard, with the "or else" lingering in the air before she goes.

It makes Beck angry.

Angry enough to defy her?

He could take Joey, walk out that door – walk for ever if he wanted to. Just *walk and walk* and forget about Germany, about the études, about his uncle he's never met and who will probably be even worse than his mother.

He slams the piano lid shut. 'Joey! We're going to the playground.'

Joey appears, still in pyjamas, with two bald Barbies. 'Really?'

'But you have to *swear* not to tell the Maestro,' he says.

'Like a secret?'

'Exactly like a secret.'

Joey's eyes shine. 'I *love you*, Beck!' She dashes off and returns in a glittery tutu over jeans and a paper crown, her hair sticking out in puffs like a mad scientist.

Beck zips on an orange striped jacket that's too tight, too short, but at least still clean and warm, and they burst out of the house into the crisp autumn afternoon.

When did he get so brave?

It's not because of August. It's because – because – of –

August. Whatever.

At the park, which hasn't been mowed in thirty years, Beck does a quick circumnavigation to ensure the shadiest of occupants are far away and look stoned and not ready to pull knives, and then he releases Joey into the wild. She shrieks and heads straight for the monkey bars.

Beck perches on a swing and waits.

And waits.

If she doesn't show up, that's a good thing, right? They'll forget about this 'debt'. She plays it tough, but she's still doing him favours. Giving him cake, inviting him places, lending him her iPod, hanging out with him when she has no need.

Joey is upside down on the monkey bars,

clutching her paper crown. 'I'M THE PRINCESS OF THE WORLD.'

Beck is glad she can't read the crude graffiti.

At least he came, right? He left the house. He did something against the Maestro. He deserves a trophy for this, or congratulatory cake. But more so the latter. He's starving.

'Oh, look!' Joey squalls, now on top of the playground tower, above the *no climbing* sign. 'Your girlfriend is coming!'

Beck's heart gives a stuttering leap before he remembers to glare at Joey like he's furious at the word *girlfriend*. Is he?

Is he?

August flies into the playground with a dazzling smile, like the knee-high grass and weeds aren't inconvenient, like she's entering the most beautiful place on earth. She holds a plastic box above her head, which promises something chocolatey. With weekend clothing freedom, she looks like a different person. She has rust-coloured shorts and a baggy crocheted jumper the colour of a Mediterranean salad. Her hair is knotted into a bandana and her bare feet – how unsurprising – are adorned with dozens of clinking metallic anklets.

'You made it!' she says. Like she's not the late one.

She slows down, panting, and flops into the

other free swing, the box on her lap. Her grin is intoxicating.

'You're going to love these, they're all gooey and ...' August pops the lid off and frowns. 'OK, I swear they looked nice before I started running.'

The cupcakes are one giant smoosh of chocolate and purple paper wrappers. August breaks off a piece and pops it in her mouth.

'They still taste good.' She shrugs and holds the box out to him.

It's polite to eat what food you're offered, right? Not because he's downright *starving*. They taste – weird. Like chocolate and – mud? But every second bite is an explosion of pure melted chocolate. And *oh* it's so good.

Joey appears at August's elbow. 'Are those for me?'

'Absolutely.'

Joey takes two and runs off again. She's halfway up the playground before she bites one and yells, 'YUCK.' And then keeps eating.

Beck winces. 'Sorry, she's—'

'Honest.' August's eyes have a wicked shine. 'There's beetroot in them.'

What.

'But the flavour grows on you, right?' August takes another bite and holds the box back out to him. A dare.

127

But *food*. He takes another misshapen cake and bites half in one go.

Joey's back at the top of the playground and demanding to be admired, so August bounces over and bubbles with dramatic praise. Joey's grin is so wide her face is in danger of splitting. How does August do that? How does she make people feel special?

It's bittersweet, actually. It reminds Beck *he's* not special. He hates himself for being like that but some of the brightness drifts out of the day.

When August returns, he twists the swing in circles and avoids eye contact.

'So,' August says, 'I had an idea of how you could repay me.'

'Did you know cake isn't supposed to have vegetables in it?'

'Oh shut up. Come over for dinner.'

She doesn't have reason to be this nice any more. Their project is done.

'You like me so much you want to eat me?' Beck says.

August rolls her eyes. 'Come and *eat* dinner *with* me and my family. Satisfied with my wording, Mister Technical?'

'I can't.'

'You say that for everything, and yet –' August spreads her arms wide and nearly falls out of her

128

swing '– here you are. I think you can be convinced.'

Why can't he just tell her? She wouldn't blab to the school. But she might look at him pityingly and – no. He's—

Embarrassed. Of his life, of the Maestro, of his weakness. He can't tell.

'Not this time,' Beck says. 'My mum is … really strict.'

'It doesn't have to be a school night.' August twists on the swing and spins around with a shriek. 'We'll make sure you eat your vegetables. I'll even walk you safely home so the bad guys don't get you.'

'Comforting,' he says. 'But I can't.'

Maybe this will be enough to make her lose interest. There's probably some other pathetic kid who needs cheering up and prodding into greatness. Although one A-scored paper probably doesn't equal *greatness*. The thought is there, anyway.

'I'M STUCK!' Joey screeches.

Beck flips out of the swing and starts toward her, but she shakes her head so madly her paper crown slips over her eyes.

'No, I want August!'

Oh.

Beck is left to the swings while August directs Joey down and then demonstrates the monkey bars – which she's too tall for and Joey too short. Beck feels a little replaced. But at least he has an excuse to watch them – well, watch August – and not be weird.

OK, it's still weird.

The dusky afternoon light is like a halo of gold around her. She deserves the halo. She's that *good*, too freaking *good*. Even when Joey stomps in a puddle and splashes mud over August's legs, she just laughs.

Good things don't last.

They walk home, each holding one of Joey's hands and swinging her over the footpath cracks. It gets dark so fast this time of year, but not dark enough that they miss seeing that half the road is covered in pears.

There's a truck with a busted axle on the side of the road, and two guys arguing.

Joey breaks free of their hands and runs to the gutter. She plucks a fat pear and spins to Beck. 'Can I eat it? Can I?'

It's like a sea of pears – squished and bruised, green and brown.

Beck hesitates, so she just bites down, grinning through the juice.

'Hey kids,' one of the truck guys calls, 'if you want those pears, take 'em.'

'Um, thanks,' Beck says.

Joey piles pears into her tutu. 'I want to eat

them all, Beck.'

August squats and plucks a few bruised ones. Half are practically pear jam where a car has driven over them.

'Do you want them?' August looks up at him. 'We have a pear tree so it's not like I need any. I can help you carry some, though.'

Picking food off the ground? She'll know how desperate he is. Although convincing Joey they don't need any would be impossible and the way she's dancing around a pile of pears proves fresh fruit is more exciting than is usual for them.

'Um,' Beck says intelligently.

August pats his shoulder. 'Stop thinking. It looks too painful for you.' She holds her huge jumper out like a basket and piles in pears.

Beck peels off his own jumper and, after blasting Joey to get off the road, he gets a dozen less mangled pears. He feels self-conscious, but the two pear deliverers don't seem to care because they're too busy trying to coax their busted truck back to life.

August sniffs a pear. 'Ooh, heavenly. These will make a delicious pie.'

Beck can think of a dozen ways to consume all these pears. First will be just gobbling them, skin and all. He can't even remember the last time he had fresh fruit.

Hauling their spoils, they trudge the last block to the Keverich house. Joey keeps cackling like a deranged chicken and shrieking 'Pears! Pears!' at random intervals.

It's only when they reach Beck's driveway that he realises he has no idea if the Maestro is home yet.

'Shall we put them in your kitchen?' August asks.

'Um, how about we just leave them out here and—'

'Beck Keverich,' August says. 'I've been in your house before and it's not a hellhole.'

'It's not that, it's just – I ...' He tries desperately to remember when the Maestro said she'd be home. Late? Early? And if she *is* home, he's already dead.

He can't get deader.

'Fine,' he mumbles and slowly opens the front door.

Joey slips under his elbow and runs inside screaming about pears. Beck can't see any signs of life, so he holds the door open for August. If she dumps the pears and runs then this might—

'Oh, hi, Mummy!' Joey says from the lounge. 'We found pears! Can we have a pie? August says we should make pie.'

No.

His insides split apart. August is in his house,

wiping her feet on the mat, oblivious to the fact he's frozen. She strolls in like she's been inside a hundred times, not just once when she was bleeding to death. He can't let her go into the kitchen alone. He jumps forward, wanting to warn her, wanting to drag her out – wanting none of this to be happening.

The Maestro and August enter the kitchen at the same time.

Beck watches a chill fury wash across the Maestro's face.

Joey chats on about pie, and August, oblivious, deposits her armful of pears on the kitchen bench. Then she wipes her hands on her shorts and, with a smile as bright as summer, she reaches out to shake hands with the Maestro.

'Hi,' she says. 'I'm August. Beck's friend.'

Beck wants to bury himself. It's over. The Maestro will blame everything on August – this trip, the reason he's started speaking up, even the lax way he's been practising. And she'll be right, of course. But this was *his*. He had something – he had something happy for once in his miserable life.

The Maestro shakes August's hand and gives a tight smile. 'How surprising,' she says. 'I didn't know Beck had a new friend.'

He wants to slam his own head into a wall.

'I'm assuming we're friends by now,' August

says. 'Scavenging pears seems a friend-sort-of-thing to do.'

'Scavenging?'

Beck clears his throat, though he'd like to turn around and walk out the door and drown himself, basically. 'Um, yeah. A truck dropped a bunch of them so we ...' He trails off. 'Anyway, this is, yeah, um, August. She's leaving now.'

August wrinkles her nose at him.

'So can we have pie?' Joey says, a pear in each hand. 'Can we have *nine* pies?'

'Hush, *Schätzchen*,' the Maestro says, because Joey is a *darling* while Beck is a *moron*. She turns back to August, still cold – in Beck's eyes – but acting disturbingly nice. 'That's very kind of you, August. How long have you been ... friends?'

'A month or so.' August smooths her stretched jumper back against her belly. 'We partnered for a paper in English. At first our relationship was *War and Peace*. Now it's *Sense and Sensibility*.'

Beck looks at her like she's grown horns.

'I'm referring to the titles,' August explains. 'It's sensible because when he sticks with me, I feed him cake and improve his grades.'

The Maestro gives a tiny laugh – how dare she – and nods. 'Beck is not a hard worker.' How *dare* she.

'Not really,' August confides. 'But once you

get past his serial killer vibe, he's just an adorable puppy.'

Beck coughs. 'Um, I'm standing right here.'

Joey has given up on being fed pie, so she drags a chair to the kitchen bench and attempts to reach the big knives. The Maestro plucks her off the chair with one strong hand and sets her down.

'Did you arrange this afternoon's picnic?' the Maestro says.

Beck says, 'No,' at the same time August says, 'Oh, we totally did.'

They look at each other. Beck's eyes try desperately to convey the *stop everything* signal. August clearly is not used to such messages.

'It's come to my attention, Mrs Keverich—' August begins.

'Ms,' the Maestro says.

'Oh, sorry. Ms Keverich – that Beck is seriously gloomy and needs kicking out of his misery.'

Joey starts kissing the pears.

'So,' August says, 'I was wondering, Ms Keverich, if Beck could come over for dinner some time?'

She's dug his grave, blissfully unaware.

The Maestro looks at Beck, long and calculating. He feels the ice, but not the burn of fury – more puzzlement, or is that shock? That he would *do* something so defiant like make a friend.

'Bee – *Beck*,' the Maestro says, unused to his nickname, 'is very busy studying.'

'Oh?' Thankfully August doesn't scoff. She probably is on the inside.

'He is a pianist,' the Maestro says, the first time she's admitted it. Usually it's *he is a worthless moron bashing my piano*. 'He has an important recital to prepare for.'

August's eyes widen with delight. 'Beck! You should've *told* me. This is incredibly exciting. I want to hear you play.'

'No,' says Beck.

'I'll take that enthusiastic response as a *yes*!' August grins. 'I'd only steal him for a few hours, Ms Keverich. I live just around the corner, and my dad could drop him home so he doesn't walk in the dark.' She pauses. 'Are you allergic to dogs, Beck?'

'No, but—'

'Great. Because there are two or twelve inside at any given time. So what do you say, Ms Keverich?'

Would she say no? Would she yell? Would she show August who she really is?

The thing about the Maestro is her ability to be purely professional around other people. In a ball gown with jewels at her throat, you'd never know there is something ... broken about this woman. She is tall and powerful and glorious.

The Maestro graciously says, 'He's facing a very taxing performance, as I said, so I will think on it.'

Beck grabs August's elbow and drags her towards the front door.

August waves over her shoulder. 'Nice meeting you, Ms Keverich.'

Beck gets her outside before he remembers how to breathe again. He wants to yell at her – he really, *really* does. But it's not like he warned her. Sure, there have been bruises – but he always says he gets into fights, accidents. Maybe she thinks that's the truth? Maybe August Frey is so full of sickening brightness that she can't fathom a parent throwing their own kid into the wall.

Beck shuts the door behind him and digs his hands through his hair. He's trying not to hyperventilate.

'Wow, Beck,' August says. 'Meeting your mum wasn't that traumatic for me. Do you want to sit down?'

He does want to sit down. Or lie down. And never get back up.

'I'm sorry,' he mumbles.

'Why?' August says. 'Your mum seems, well, fierce but not too bad. I get that she's strict though. Wow.'

'No,' Beck whispers, 'I'm sorry for this.' He sucks in air, strength, and then looks her in the eyes. 'We're done, OK? We did the paper, so you don't need to come around any more.'

August looks at him steadily.

'I don't *need* a friend,' Beck says. 'I actually don't *want* one.' Life was less painful when he didn't know what he was missing. 'So – so leave me alone, OK?' Please.

Will she demand an answer? Slink off like he kicked her? Lash out because he's unfair?

There's a stagnant pause and then –

She laughs and punches his shoulder. 'You're messed up, kid. But, you're also stuck with me, and a super-scary mum isn't going to send me screaming.'

He groans. 'August, I'm not kidding around—'

'Neither am I, but I do have to go.' She backs away, thumbs tucked in her pockets. 'I meant it when I said I want to hear you play!'

'Absolutely not,' Beck yells after her.

She turns, ready to sprint off her excess energy. 'That's how you can repay me! Write me a song. Then we'll be even.'

Write *her* a song? What – no –

She takes off down the road, the twilight swallowing her before he can reply and he's left standing in the cold with a mouthful of words he can't say.

He doesn't want to go inside, but –

The Maestro is waiting, her eyes cold, calm. Beck shuts the door and leans on it, ready but not ready, angry but tired.

The Maestro looks at him, *really* looks, like she hasn't in a long time. Then she shakes her head and laughs.

It's a terrible sound.

'It won't last long,' she says. 'Especially after you leave for *Deutschland*.'

CHAPTER 12

The unfortunate thing about being fifteen is growing taller. Beck tries to stop, for the sake of fitting his clothes, but his body doesn't listen.

He attempts to disappear behind the $10 clothes racks while the Maestro flips through and scrutinises the colours. Joey is impersonating a tornado and has knocked hangers off shelves, dismantled the shoe aisle and is currently clomping around in men's gumboots that come to her thighs while wearing a straw hat.

'We should just go,' Beck whispers to no one who cares.

The Maestro yanks a black and yellow striped polo shirt off the rack. Everything she does is fast and angry and vicious, like the clothing has particularly insulted her. 'What about this?'

Does he want to look like a bumblebee? 'Not really my, um, *style*.'

The Maestro concedes and puts it back. 'What you need, *Sohn*, is a haircut.'

He likes his hair, though, the way it looks like an electrified steel scourer. And he can't imagine the Maestro paying for a barber *and* clothes, which leaves her to do the trimming and – basically, *no*.

It's weird enough clothes shopping with her. Her rage has burned to embers and, yes, the smoulders are ready to flare, but they can actually walk through the shops without imminent fear of doom. It's his uncle that's done this. Jan Keverich. Which makes no sense since the Maestro seemed to hate him and his success enough to *leave* Germany in the first place – but maybe it's the thought of home, of shooting Beck to stardom, of finally *succeeding*, that makes her happy.

Happy? He shouldn't throw that word around so easily. Happy is August. Not-destroying-something-momentarily is the Maestro.

'I don't need a haircut,' Beck says. 'It's the Keverich trademark.'

The Maestro grunts. 'Well stop sulking and go find a shirt.'

A shirt to replace the one smudged with blood.

Beck half wishes he could just wear it, *prove* something, and use this money to buy a fat steak and an ice cream sandwich for once. Instead the Maestro chooses to notice he's grown and decides to do something about it.

The Maestro shakes out a black button-down shirt.

'Great,' Beck says. 'Buy it and let's go.'

The Maestro squints at it and picks at a piece of fluff. 'The quality is rubbish. And not – not …' She glares at the clothes, searching for the word. 'Not *enough*.'

Enough for *what*? To prove they're not dirt poor?

For the first time, Beck actually wonders if she wants him to look nice in front of his uncle because she's ashamed. Of all of them.

Beck slinks off to pretend to inspect socks. He has a strange knot in his chest – probably because he's out with the Maestro, right? Definitely. Not because she seems, despite her size taking up half the store, somehow … *frail*.

He glances at her, between socks, as she drops the black shirt, picks it up, drops it, and then stabs the coat hanger at the neck hole with shaking hands.

No. He refuses to feel sorry for her.

Beck finds plastic packets of cheap white shirts and he selects his size. When he returns, the

Maestro holds mustard jeans and a black and grey knitted jumper. Beck resists the urge to flee.

'Dressing rooms,' she barks. 'Now.'

Trying clothes is complicated because Beck is swallowed by the male side while the Maestro waits outside, and he hates the thought of parading in the open in strange clothes. What is wrong with normal-coloured jeans anyway? But these fit, tighter than the baggy trousers he's used to, and the jumper is soft, if a little big, and encases him in the warmest hug he's had in years.

He slinks out, twisting to see the price tags.

'How much does this—'

The Maestro cuts him off with her voice as bold as an orchestra. '*Gut*,' she says.

Good? She said *good* in relation to *him*?

Beck forgets he's trying to grab the price tag behind his neck.

Joey, bouncing at the Maestro's side, pauses to survey him. 'Wow.'

Beck sighs.

The Maestro motions to the jeans. 'Too tight? Too loose?'

Despite the unaccustomed tightness, they feel – good. 'They fit.'

'Comfortable?' the Maestro prods.

'I guess.' Beck's so confused. Why is she caring? What is she *doing* this for?

Joey pokes him. 'Does the tag say nine and three?'

'What?' Beck spins and catches the price tag. $39. Why is she insisting on spending so much on clothes? 'We can't – I can't—'

The Maestro tells Joey to hush.

Panic rises in his throat. 'What's going on? Why do I need expensive clothes?'

The Maestro folds her arms to stop her shaking hands. 'It's no crime to have something nice in your wardrobe.'

'I'm hungry.' Joey starts to wilt. 'I'm *so hungry*.'

'No lunch until we're done here,' the Maestro says.

Joey folds her arms, bottom lip out.

'But what are *the clothes for*?' Beck grits his teeth, aware he's spoken too loud.

The ice in the Maestro's eyes is warning.

'Sorry,' he mumbles. 'But please …'

The Maestro grabs Joey's hand. 'We'll take them,' she says, briskly.

In the changing room, Beck whips off the clothes, cursing them and his mother, and even Joey for fraying the Maestro's nerves when she was in a semi-good mood. He slips into his holey hoody and baggy jeans, rocking the homeless look, and then glares at the three full-length mirrors. Only a skinny, angry idiot scowls back.

If she's buying him nice clothes, maybe she plans to pack him off to Germany with or without Jan's blessing. Maybe she's happy because she can see the end of his irritating presence in sight.

He stalks out and tosses the jeans, jumper and new white suit shirt in her basket. Her money. Who cares? She can waste it on some freaking clothes.

They move towards the checkouts, both the Maestro and Beck taking turns to make sure Joey isn't stuffing shiny items in her pockets.

'There will be a lesson,' the Maestro says, finally.

'I thought it was a performance.'

'*Ja und nein*. First there's a performance at an acquaintance of Jan's mansion. A small detour from his main tour.'

Mansion? Rich people.

'Then,' the Maestro says, 'a lesson. For Jan to assess you. We've spoken and arranged this.'

'But—' Beck stops. He shouldn't carry on – but they're in an open place. Not like she can slap him. 'But I don't want to go to Germany.'

The Maestro appears not to have heard. She pauses by a rack of frilly little girl clothes. Glittery stockings and pink tees that say 'Daddy's Princess'. Currently, Joey's wearing clothes from a second-hand sale – red jumper, polka dot leggings and pink glitter gumboots.

'You do not understand the opportunity.' The Maestro's lips curl. 'To learn from the greatest? To make something of yourself? You could be as great as me – perhaps. I thought you might try, *Schwachkopf.*'

Beck flushes. 'I'm your kid. You can't just sell me—'

The Maestro waves her hand sharply, done with him. 'Take your sister and wait outside.'

All he can do drag Joey towards the exit while she says, 'It's not *fair*, I didn't get a present!' with a five-year-old's righteous indignation.

'I know, Joey,' Beck says, soothing. 'It's not fair.'

He doesn't want to do well at the performance. He doesn't want to impress Jan.

He doesn't want to leave.

CHAPTER 13

The air smiles with winter teeth – an official welcome to *time-for-your-hands-to-freeze-on-the-piano* season. Joy.

Beck stuffs his fingers beneath his armpits as he and August trudge to school. She's jacketless and shoeless as usual, and mildly blue. She rubs her arms and bounces on the spot while Beck disappears into the noisy chaos of paint and dress-ups to bodily remove his little sister as she shouts at the teacher and stomps her small feet in fury. The teacher's face is plum, and she's ready to throw Joey at him. There's also a letter.

Joey's been suspended.

The *preschooler* has been suspended.

Even Beck hasn't fallen that low yet, though he's never turned in complete homework in his life. No one expects much from him. But tossing the cherubic, big-eyed five-year-old out? He's furious.

'She's a *meanie*,' Joey howls, as Beck drags her out by the hood of her red coat. 'She didn't listen. I'm not a liar. I'm *not*! I'm a *good* girl.'

Beck stuffs the letter into his backpack, half wishing he could rip it and toss the pieces in that pedantic teacher's face.

'What did you even do?' August seems curious instead of shocked.

'Who cares? No one should suspend a preschooler,' Beck says, harsher than he intended.

August commences a round of jumping jacks while Beck buttons Joey's coat.

'I got expelled from a preschool once,' she says. 'This kid found a bird half drowned in the water tank, so he used a plastic shovel to "put it out of its misery". Seriously, the bird was *not* dead. He murdered it and had its blood on his *shoes*.'

Joey's eyes went wide. 'What did you do?'

August pauses and Beck isn't sure if her cheeks are flushed with cold or embarrassment.

When she doesn't answer, he nudges her. 'What *did* you do?'

'I might've bashed him with the same shovel,' August confesses. 'He might've had to get nine stitches. Look, I'm not *proud* of it. I retaliate peacefully now—'

'Like with the frog,' Beck reminds her, 'and that guy you kicked.'

August shrugs. 'I possibly have a mild violent streak. At least the last dude didn't have to get stitches. While I, on the other hand, lost a toenail and nearly bled dramatically to death.'

Beck is actually impressed. August's never going to be bulldozed in her righteous fights. She'll be the one chained to a tree for three months to stop it being chopped down, or in prison for maiming hunters.

They start off down the footpath, Beck in awed silence, August embarrassed and Joey with her head hung low in dejection.

'All I did was call Bailey a *Scheisskerl*,' Joey mumbles, 'and then I bit her nose.'

'You *bit* her?' Beck's jaw drops. 'You're not a baby, Joey. What is this?'

'She said my mummy doesn't love me because she never brings me to school!' Joey says. 'Then she broke my crayons. *All* of them. Even the *glitter crimson*. And I'm never, ever, *ever* going to get new crayons because – because ...' She stops, hiccupping through her tears.

Because the Maestro won't care enough to buy more. He knows. As much as the Maestro

149

occasionally cares about Joey, she doesn't lavish affectionate gifts on her. And Beck understands the specialness of *glitter crimson* since he got kicked for attempting to use it while colouring companionably with her.

Beck is helpless in the face of justified rage. 'You still shouldn't have bitten her,' he manages.

August bounces over a crack in the cement footpath. 'What would you have done, Beck?'

Is she messing with him? He glances at her, but she looks *serious*, as if she's genuinely unsure what the right thing to do in this devastating situation is. Maybe August sides with Joey.

'Probably nothing.' Beck isn't proud of the answer. But what else can he say? He can't encourage Joey, but he knows full well how incriminating Joey can look. Loud, brash, mouthy and physical? The teacher informed Beck that if his mother wouldn't come in to talk about Joey's long list of bad behaviours, then she had no choice but to suspend Joey.

'EVERYONE IS MEAN TO ME!' Joey wails. 'Mama doesn't love me, and Bailey is just a—'

Beck covers her mouth. 'Joey, please. August was innocent before we met her.'

August nods. 'Not any more. Joey's got quite a tongue.'

Joey tries to bite Beck's hand, so he retracts.

Beck claws deep inside himself for something encouraging to say, even though his mind is spinning to what the Maestro's going to *do* with Joey when she has to work and Beck goes to school. 'Well, Mama does love you.' Definitely. A lot more than her son, anyway.

After all, Joey hasn't been forced on to the piano yet.

She hunches in her coat. 'Then I want new crayons.'

August laughs. 'You're extraordinary, Joey. You really ought to be a superhero or the queen someday.'

Joey considers this. 'Superhero,' she says. 'I want to smash things.'

She breaks into a run, pelting towards the end of the street and into the Keverich hovel, slamming the front door after her. It gives Beck a moment of peace with August. Not that he needs it, of course. It's just August. She's just ... some random school acquaintance.

August is still smiling to herself, like Joey is the most glorious creation in the world. She rubs her hands together and blows on them. Beck wonders what it'd be like to hold her hand. Sweaty? Frozen? Would their fingers fit or would it be awkward?

'Have you started writing my song?' she says.

He has. He's also abandoned every rubbish

attempt. He has to work on it in small sporadic bursts so the Maestro won't notice it isn't Chopin.

Nothing he composes will be good enough for August.

'No way,' he says. 'I told you, there is zero possibility of you hearing me play.'

August sticks out her bottom lip – it's slightly blue. 'You break my heart, Keverich. How about dinner? Did your mum give the affirmative?'

They haven't even raised the subject since.

He shrugs.

'You're talkative today,' August says. 'Something eating your brain?'

Only a few things. Small things. He could be shipped off to Germany in a few weeks to live with an uncle who's possibly *worse* than his mother. Or he could be strangled by the Maestro if he messes up. He could lose Joey. He could lose—

He shrugs again.

They pause on the driveway. The curtain flickers – Joey or the Maestro, he doesn't know – and he can't linger. But he *wants* to. Lingering isn't half so awkward and emptying as saying goodbye.

'Why do you always run?' he blurts out suddenly. 'After you leave here?'

August looks startled. 'What? Oh. I don't know.' She chews her lip. 'To feel alive, I guess? Don't you want to run after sitting in stuffy

152

classrooms for six hours? Don't you want to do *something* to remember that you are a person, not a test score?'

No.

Never.

He wouldn't even *dare*.

'I guess.' It doesn't sound convincing even to him.

He hates how innocent her face is, how her lips are twisted in a quiet smile, how her breath puffs in globes of cold white. He hates it because she is *hope* and *tomorrow* and he's a *goodbye* and *the end*.

She leans close, the warmth of her breath on his cheek – yeasty, because she ate sourdough bread for lunch after offering him a piece. He refused. His cornflake sandwich was so much better, obviously.

'Write my song about being *alive*,' she says.

'It's not going to have lyrics.' Great. He just admitted he's working on it.

'What kind of song is it? Wait – oh *wait*.' Her eyes sparkle wickedly, like she's just eaten the best joke. 'You don't play *classical* piano, do you, Keverich?'

'No,' he growls.

She tips back her head and hoots to the frosty sky. 'Classical! My mum would be in love with you. *Classical.*' She steps back, hands on her hips, and looks him up and down. 'You are a scrawny, bitter, nasty *classical* pianist and I don't know whether that's the best thing I've ever heard or just the funniest.'

'Ha, ha. I'm dying of laughter here.'

Her eyes glint. 'Someday I'll do something extraordinarily spontaneous and you'll learn how to smile.'

'Yeah? Like what?'

She whirls and Beck half expects wings made of frost and longing to sprout from her back and fly her home. He wants to catch her, pin the wings *just for a second* and ask to fly with her. Ask to be saved.

'Oh, who could know?' she shouts over her shoulder, running down the street. 'Maybe I'll kiss you.'

She's gone. The golden afternoon swallows her and leaves Beck at the end of his driveway more confused than if she'd slapped him.

Did she mean it?

Is she –

no.

They don't have that kind of relationship. They're barely *friends* now and she's just messing with him, friend-to-friend style.

Or she likes him.

He *cannot* think about that.

Realising he also can't spend the rest of his day staring off down the street, he goes inside. It's probably a throwaway remark. She probably kisses all the boys she meets, just to see how kissable they are. He wouldn't be kissable. He's piano keys and flinches and crumpled music trapped in his soul. Not kissable. Kickable.

The Maestro is home. Worse, she's actually cooking dinner. From the mounds of potato peels and the applesauce brewing on the stove, it must be *Kartoffelpuffer* – potato pancakes. A hot, homemade meal instead of frozen fish cakes for once?

He stares for a minute as she struggles with a potato and a knife. It slips in her shaking hands and slices her finger. Cursing, she jams it in her mouth and turns to see him.

'I can, um, peel them for you,' Beck says.

Surprisingly, the Maestro steps back and jabs a finger at the stack of potatoes. '*Ja*, be useful.'

He could be a lot more useful around the house if he wasn't practising the freaking piano all day.

Beck dumps his backpack and remembers the letter. He's betraying her, but what can he do? She's *five*. Joey's forgotten her disgrace and sits in front of the TV.

'Um, this is from Joey's teacher.'

The Maestro raises her eyebrows and accepts it. Beck busies himself with the potatoes and knife and pretends not to notice how long it takes her to open it. Her hands have definitely gotten worse.

She sucks in a sharp breath. '*Verdammt nochmal*. Johanna!'

Joey slinks into the kitchen.

'She said she bit some kid,' Beck says.

'*Ja*, and the teacher too.' The Maestro looks shocked – an unusual change from her normal scowl. 'She swore violently at a student and *threatened them with scissors*. Then bit the teacher intervening and hit repeatedly—' The Maestro breaks off, nostrils flaring.

Joey goes boneless and flops, face first, on the floor.

Fear crawls into Beck's throat. What if – no. The Maestro can't possibly punish Joey when *she* is the reason Joey's so violent. The Maestro has to see that, right? He ducks his head and peels potatoes fast.

'This is not how you behave, Johanna.' The Maestro slams the letter against the bench. 'This is *beschämend*.' Disgraceful.

Joey raises her head a fraction off the tiles and gives a pterodactyl screech.

The Maestro doesn't bat an eyelid. 'Go to your room, go on, naughty girl! No television. You stay

156

in your room until dinner. Go.'

Beck flips potato peels into the sink and tries not to sag with relief.

Joey kicks her feet, but a few sharp words from the Maestro has her picking herself up and running in a whirlwind of childhood fury to her room. She slams her door.

Beck hacks chunks off his potatoes. If the Maestro didn't swear at him, Joey wouldn't—

'It is my fault,' says the Maestro.

Beck drops the knife and it clatters in the sink. He stares at her.

The Maestro leans heavily against the bench, her enormous frame looking tired and completely done. Even her normally wild hair just droops about her ears.

'If you didn't try my patience so—' The Maestro stops again and sighs deeply. Then she leans over the sauce and gives it a stir.

Yes, blame him. Totally fair.

Beck scoops the peel into the bin and starts to slink away, but the Maestro holds up a hand.

'Wait.'

Here it comes. A blasting because somehow everything is always Beck's fault.

'You and I need to talk – about this girl.'

'Girl?' Heat rises up Beck's neck.

Joey's bedroom door pops open. 'Do you mean

August? August is my *bestest* of *best* friend. And she's Beck's girlfriend.'

'To your room!' the Maestro barks.

Growling, Joey slams her door again.

'She's not my girlfriend,' Beck says, desperately. He's not discussing this. Ever. With anyone. 'There's nothing—'

'Bah.' The Maestro hefts a huge knife from the drawer and starts slicing onions. 'The window was open. I heard.'

She's *spying* on him? She controls his whole freaking life, and she needs to have this too?

'She meets you for school every day,' the Maestro goes on. 'That girl is your fifth limb.'

'She's just a friend,' Beck says, struggling to keep his voice even. 'I want a friend. I'm practising—'

'You call that *schreckliche Lärm* practising?' The Maestro snorts, but at least these insults are usual and Beck doesn't blink. 'But this is not about practice.' Her knife slams against the board. 'Although friends are distractions from the piano, which is not good. Not good at all. When a boy distracted me, my career nearly collapsed – and I got pregnant with you.' With a *snick* her knife beheads another onion.

'I'm sorry,' Beck says bitterly.

'Never mind that,' the Maestro says, oblivious

to the sarcasm. 'The problem was the distraction. My music was nothing to me when he was on my mind. Notes disappeared and all I saw was his eyes, his smile.'

This is the most she's talked about Beck's father.

She slams the knife down. 'He was too jealous of the piano, always too jealous. Even after my hands ...' Her voice roughens. 'He did not come back, the *Schwein*. Those without music in their bones are not to be trusted.'

No music? Sounds like paradise.

'That girl,' the Maestro says, '*August*. She does not love you. She loves broken things.'

Beck's eyes snap to hers.

'It's obvious, *Schwachkopf*.' The Maestro scoops the chopped onions into a bowl. 'The way she dresses, her hippy hair –' she says it with a sneer '– the way she fawns over you.'

'She doesn't.'

'Don't be blind,' she snaps.

Emotion strains the Maestro's voice, and Beck can't understand it. He can't understand this entire conversation.

'She is the kind of girl,' the Maestro says, 'who falls in love with a broken toy, but once it's fixed, she moves on. She wants to "save" you.' She drips with bitterness. 'No doubt you've painted me the monster. Well, fine. I shall be your monster. But I will also get you into the greatest concert halls in the world, get you the best tutor, make your name be known, make you a famous pianist who will want for nothing. Your little girlfriend will take that away.'

Stop it. *Stop it*.

'This August is … sweet.' The Maestro probably chokes on the word. 'But you are her project for happiness, not something real. You are a puppy to cuddle. So stop. Be done with this. You are like me and relationships are not for us.'

He's not like the Maestro. He's not. He's – not?

Except …

The times he punched the wall so his knuckles bled, the macabre fantasies of chopping off his hands, the way he loses hours in the music he claims to hate, the way he wanted to kill that bully …

'And you are going to Germany.' The Maestro gets out an egg, flour, butter for the potato pancakes. 'Here is advice you need to learn, *Junge*. If you do not say hello, you do not need to say goodbye.'

He hates her in that moment, utterly hates her. When she doesn't say anything else, he walks away, fighting fear that she's right. She can't be right. August isn't – but she is. A rescuer. A fixer.

A saviour. And that's why he likes her, isn't it?

'The *Kartoffelpuffer* will be ready for those who practise hard,' the Maestro calls out.

As if he's hungry.

Beck wants to punch a hole through his chest and rip out his own stupid heart. Why did he think he could get away with being near August? He doesn't deserve her, anyway – not the happiness, the kindness, not the way her smile rubs off on him, or the flippant promise of a kiss.

He is like the Maestro. Why would he want to inflict himself on August?

Beck shuts his door – quietly – and slides on to the piano stool. The keys stare at him, blank, cold, unforgiving.

He just wanted a friend. A real friend.

One

single

friend.

His fingers crash against the keys so hard the room shakes around him. He hammers the Chopin with hate, hate, *hate*. Every single note of agony and fury and suffocating despair.

And when his door cracks open, and he's ready to scream at the intruder, the Maestro appears. She nods at him, just once. '*Gut gemacht*,' she says. *Good job*. 'Now come for dinner.'

He could cry.

He's waited for the words *good job* for so long. But now that they're finally given, he can only hold them in tired, hollow hands and hate himself for craving them so desperately.

But he doesn't cry. He unchains himself from his eighty-eight keys and eats dinner and does the dishes, and speaks politely, and understands that the Maestro plays a mind game with him. But maybe she won't win this time?

When he closes his eyes that night, he composes August's song.

CHAPTER 14

There's a wall of ice between Beck and August, ice with doubt taped over the cracks. Every time Beck snatches a glance at her, he's not sure what he sees any more. The August of trees and coconut and bare feet is blurred with the August who's only interested in rescuing broken things. Either way, he'll have to say goodbye to her one day. Maybe it should be now.

It's easier than he thought. He suddenly has nothing to say.

At first, August doesn't notice the ice, the silence. Although, on the second day, she stops pummelling jabs and quips at him and just walks in silence. It's a heavy silence. Her walk lacks its usual bounce, she keeps stealing swift glances at him, and she doesn't hum any Twice Burgundy melodies under her breath.

Beck should be relieved.

Pretty soon she'll wander back to her real friends. Or she'll adopt another battered kid in the class and feed them sesame crackers and do their homework. She'll move on.

With Joey still suspended on the third day, Beck nearly walks home alone.

Well, he tries.

August is also a fast runner.

She catches up with him, satchel rattling with her ever-present collection of Sharpies. She falls into step beside him. 'Hey there, Beck.'

They haven't spoken today. Why break it now? Beck shrugs and keeps walking. There's a knife in his throat.

'You're angry,' she says.

'No.'

'Ah, of course. This is how you treat all your friends.'

Beck gestures to the empty footpath around them. '*Ja*. This is why I have *so many friends*.'

It's bitter, sharp enough that they fall into silence again. August's shoes make a flapping-slap sound, like her soles need gluing. Since he recreationally stares at the ground, he focuses on her broken shoes, not her face, and notices she's doodled over her legs today. Compasses and lists of cities. *Paris. Rio. Kuala Lumpur.*

Maybe she would visit him in Germany ...

Stop.

Don't think like that. It's not worth it.

'This is about what I said the other day.' August's voice is unusually quiet, but not timid.

'What?' Beck knows exactly what.

'About kissing you.' She looks up, unabashed, unashamed. 'I meant it, but I can also get over it if girls aren't your thing.'

His face burns.

'No.' His tongue is in nineteen knots. 'It's not – that's not it. It's – I mean. I *like* girls but not—'

'Don't say "but not you",' August says. 'You'll break my heart.'

'I wasn't going to say that.' Yes he was! Why is he still talking? Shut up, you idiot! 'Doesn't matter. Forget it.' He walks faster.

'I won't.' August keeps up easily. 'We've got to get this sorted before my birthday.'

'Your birthday? But it's only July.'

'Yes, you genius. My birthday is in July.'

'But isn't your birthday in, um, August?'

August groans to the heavens. 'No! My parents aren't *that* bad.'

'So who are you named after? Augustus Caesar Salad?'

'Firstly,' August says, holding up a finger to tick off her points, 'Augustus Caesar is *not* a salad, and secondly, I'm not named after *anyone*, my mum liked the name, and thirdly—'

'Please let there only be three points.'

'There are *nine* points, but you're so deplorable I'll stop after three.' She sniffs, put out. '*Thirdly.* "August" means majestic, and my parents want me to sit on a throne eventually.' She elbows him in the ribs. 'Why are you called "Beck"? Your mum wanted a Rebecca?'

Beck doesn't talk about his full name. No one does. It's the most off-limits conversation in the entire universe. But knowing August? She's not going to leave this alone. In fact, while his silence stretches, she rips up a piece of long grass as they walk and tickles him behind the ear.

He snatches it off her.

'Beck is my nickname.' That's all he's giving.

'Short for Beckett? Or Beckham? Becker?'

'No.'

'Don't make me threaten you,' August warns. 'Because I have *so much* blackmail material and I can also kick really hard and – oh! Remember when I gave you cake? You owe me.'

Beck's voice folds into a whisper. 'Beethoven.'

'Sorry? What was that?' August cups a hand to her ear. 'I could've sworn you said—'

'BEETHOVEN BLOODY KEVERICH.' He yells it straight in her ear so she winces and nearly falls into the gutter. He gets a small amount of satisfaction from that.

August stops, her mouth drops, and she just stares at him. He hesitates, fingering his backpack straps. She wouldn't – no, because August is *nice*, she's not going to—

She doubles up and cracks up laughing.

Beck takes everything back. She is not nice.

'Are you serious?' she squawks. 'Beethoven? Your name is literally *Beethoven*? And you're a *pianist*? Did your parents *hate* you or plan this or—'

'Shut up.' He takes off, walking fast.

She's laughing too hard to even walk straight, so she stumbles along behind him, wiping her eyes. Finally, the snorts subsiding, she dances to his side.

'Well, *Beethoven* –' she pauses to giggle, so he shoves her, harder this time, and she ducks away '– you've gotten me so off track. I was talking about my birthday before that beautiful reveal.'

'If you call me Beethoven *ever again*,' he growls, 'I'll throttle you.'

'You do have large hands,' she agrees. 'But no friends to help you bury a body.' She fakes a pout.

'So sad, little Beethoven. You're destined to put up with me.'

This sends her into another howl of laughter, and it's nearly a minute before she's composed enough to whip an envelope out of her satchel and smack it in his face.

'This is for you,' she says. 'You have to come, by the way, because I'm turning sixteen and that's a huge deal.'

Isn't sixteen for kissing boys and driving cars and deciding on your future of possibilities? It would be for August. For him? The only possibility is a lifetime of diminished sevenths. His birthday isn't until October, which is far enough away to make him feel miserably young next to August.

'Is this a party invitation?' Beck says warily.

'Yes.' August smiles dreamily. 'Only a small crowd, *very* small, since everyone is terrified of my dogs. Or my parents. Who knows.' She pauses to roll her eyes. 'And my mum's making a vegan cake—'

'Ugh.'

'You'll love it.' She punches his arm. 'And you'll love my parents and also my nine dogs.'

'Wait. Nine?'

'I told you we run a shelter.' August shrugs. 'We don't put down animals, we rescue them. And if they don't find homes, I home them. I work weekends to pay for their food, but saving animals is the most incredible gift I can give this universe.'

Beck wishes he could work weekends and give Joey the chocolates and sparkly hairclips she craves. He taps the envelope against his thigh and envisions the Maestro laughing as she tears it up.

'There will be epic music,' August says, 'and star gazing. You don't even have to stay long. Like, just an hour. Or even just thirty minutes. I'll make you up a little doggy bag of cake.'

An hour without the Maestro knowing where he is? Never going to happen.

They're at his house now, and he's not sure if he wants to run inside and bolt the door, or procrastinate as long as possible. Everything to do with August is complicated.

'I'll try,' Beck says. He won't.

'Great!' August spins around him. 'And we're good now, right? No more of this awkward silence?'

Are they OK? Does it *matter* what she thinks of him? Does it matter that she isn't bashful about mentioning a kiss? Does it matter if August does exactly the opposite of everything he thinks she'll do?

Her impossible eyes are on him now, waiting, wanting to understand something she never can.

She dances in a world of possibilities, and he drowns in music.

'I d-do like, um, girls. I like you.' It's coming out so completely mashed; he's mortified. Why is he even talking? Shut up and go *inside*. 'Um, but – not – I just mean. I like you but normally. Friends. Yeah, like friends. Not … more.' *Verdammt*, he's so embarrassed.

August puts a hand on her hip. 'Hmm. I see how it is. I'll need to work on this.' She turns to leave and then, her eyes blazing with inspiration, she dashes back to him, rises on tiptoes and whispers in his ear, 'I like you too, Beethoven.' Then she runs down the road and he swears he hears her laugh again.

She enjoys this, doesn't she?

He tells himself he does *not* enjoy it. *And, by the way, Beck, there is no way you're going to a party after the Maestro's recent analysis of August.*

Still, he breaks open the envelope as he enters his house, and skims the details. *Celebrate August Frey's 16th. Starts at 6 p.m. Don't bring anything except your happy self.* He clearly shouldn't be invited.

Still reading, he kicks the front door shut and walks smack into the Maestro.

She plucks the letter from his hand. Beck winces. Being stuck in the house all day with Joey is *not* improving her temperament. 'What is this?'

'It's just a party,' Beck says, feebly. 'I-I don't

have to go.' *But I want to.*

'August.' The Maestro rolls her eyes and slaps the invitation back in his hand. 'Didn't we talk about this, *Schwachkopf?* Throw it out and go practise. No dinner until the Chopin is acceptable.'

Beck doesn't answer. He crumples the invitation in his fist and reminds himself she didn't say *no*. And that's a positive, right?

The piano glares at him. He tosses his school bag, changes clothes, and begins scales.

He's ready to play for his uncle. He's *ready*. But still he goes over and over and over the études, trying to focus and ignore his own music in his head begging to be played. He only considers stopping to stretch his fingers for the briefest second when—

He hears Joey shriek.

Beck breaks off the piece abruptly, frowning. Is it just a tantrum about the TV or Joey unleashing her energy after being home with her mother for three days? It's dark outside, past when they should've eaten dinner – obviously he's not playing 'acceptably' yet – so maybe Joey's having a hungry meltdown.

Still.

He hates to hear his sister cry.

Beck nudges his bedroom door open and creeps into the hall. He can smell bratwurst sausage and

171

garlic and caraway. So clearly dinner is happening, just not for *him*.

'I DON'T WANT TO,' Joey hollers.

Beck strolls into the kitchen, trying to look nonchalant. He gets a glass from the cupboard and pours himself water.

'Mind your tone with me, *Göre*,' the Maestro snaps.

Brat? What happened to *darling* and *sweetie*, her usual terms of endearment for her favourite child? This scares Beck.

She sits at her table before a plate of sausage, mashed potato and sauerkraut, her arms folded. At first Beck thinks she must be whingeing about the food. But then the Maestro points towards Beck's open bedroom door and the corner of the shiny Steinway piano.

'It is a privilege to play the piano,' the Maestro says.

Beck clutches his glass and forgets to drink.

'And to be a Keverich is to *play*,' she says. 'To play music is to learn discipline and have direction and purpose. You are no *kleines Kind* any more.'

Joey's face is as red as the Maestro's. 'No!' she shouts. 'I hate it. I don't wanna play all day, I want to be a chef and a mermaid and—'

'*Nein*. You will learn.' The Maestro stabs at her sausage. She sees Beck and her furious eyes land on him. 'Have you finished your practice?' Her tone is sharper than the sauerkraut.

'No,' Beck says. 'I just – I'm hungry …' *I want to rescue Joey from you.*

'Food is for those who play well.' The Maestro throws her cutlery down and rises. 'That goes for you too, Johanna. If you refuse the piano, you refuse dinner.'

Joey drops her own pink plastic fork. 'I *hate* the piano. It's noisy and mean. And I *hate* how Beck plays when I wanna sleep.' She hiccups. 'I won't play the mean piano. No, no, NO.'

She slides off her chair, ready to run, but the Maestro grabs her elbow.

The Maestro scowls venom at Beck. 'This is all your fault, *Schwachkopf*. You've poisoned her to me.'

Beck doesn't think. He just speaks. 'Joey's too young, *Mutter*. She shouldn't have to—'

'She should do what I say!' roars the Maestro. 'As should you.'

Joey squirms in her grip. 'No, no, no. *Ich hasse dich*. I hate you!'

The Maestro slaps her.

She's never struck Joey – usually it's not-so-subtle hints of what might happen if Beck doesn't fold to the Maestro's will. But she never actually *hits her*. Joey is the thing he cares most about in this upside-down world. But the Maestro lashing out at a kid while Beck stays quiet? He can't slink away and let her rage.

So Beck, who does nothing, does something.

He moves like a wraith, grabbing Joey as she goes boneless against the Maestro, and pushes her behind him. He throbs with rage, *disgust*, that she'd let loose on a five-year-old.

'She's just a little kid.' Beck's teeth are clenched.

Purple veins bulge in the Maestro's neck. 'You started when you were younger than—'

And you want her to end up like me? Beck tries to keep his voice level. 'There's only one piano anyway and Joey can't even sit still and she probably can't—'

The Maestro hits him.

The blow sends him stumbling away from Joey and he just *hopes* the Maestro didn't use that kind of force on her. Joey's on the floor now, quiet, wide-eyed. Trembling.

Joey is made for glitter crowns and robots constructed with yogurt boxes and muddy puddles and untamed hair. She is not made for the piano.

'You are a disappointment.' The Maestro's teeth are gritted. 'You fail me on purpose, I know it, *du nutzloser Junge*. Mayhap my daughter will try harder to carry my legacy.'

'I do try,' Beck says. He should shut up, but –

this time? This time is so, so different. 'I swear, I *do*. I'm just not good enough.'

'No,' she says coldly. 'You're not. You are a disgrace to my name. You play for hours a day and what do I hear? *Rubbish!* I'm sickened by the very sound of your mistakes. And yet you cannot do better – *nein*. You do not *try* to do better.'

Beck tells himself he doesn't care. He doesn't, doesn't – *doesn't*—

'I wanted a prodigy. And what did I get? You. *You worthless disappointment*.' The Maestro snatches her plate of half-eaten sausage and potatoes and flings it against the wall. Food makes a wet splatter. Crockery shatters.

Joey scoots forward and hugs Beck's leg. 'Don't hurt him,' she whimpers.

The Maestro grabs the vase of pebbles and fake flowers from the bench top. She slams that against the wall too, but doesn't let go, so glass bites her flesh. Blood flows. Beck backs away as shards rain across his arms. She's lost it. She's – this can't – no.

'Go to your room, Jo,' he whispers, prying her off his leg.

'Did I say you could leave?' the Maestro screams.

'I'm sorry.' He has nothing else to say.

'SORRY IS NOT ENOUGH ANY MORE.' The Maestro is gone, *gone*, deep into the agony of ruined hands and abandonment and frothing hate.

But she can still hit.

She grabs Beck by the throat of his shirt and rams him into the wall. He's not a plate. He doesn't shatter. But the wind goes out of him in a *whoosh*.

Her fist connects with his jaw.

It's OK, Beck, just go away, go somewhere else in your head. Where's your music? Find your music. Better you than Joey, right? Right.

Or stand up –

fight?

Beck shoves the Maestro away. Hard.

The surprise on her face is matched by the catastrophic pounding of his heart. He's going to regret that. Her eyes are too white, her face discoloured, her hands trembling violently.

'She's not playing the piano,' Beck says, ragged. 'If you try, I'll smash the piano. I swear I'll smash that *gottverdammte* piano.'

But his voice trembles, and how can you take a wavering threat seriously?

'I sacrificed everything for that piano,' the Maestro shouts. '*Everything*, you ungrateful brat. The thousands I needed for therapy on my hands, I spent on you. *Thousands!*' She slaps him for emphasis. 'So you would have a future. You will play, you will—'

'Maybe I don't want to.' What is he doing? He's bitten his tongue and his mouth is full of blood.

Stop. *Stop talking*. But there is a crack across his soul and something red and vicious and desperate crawls out. 'Maybe I hate the piano too. But you never ask. You *never care*. You hate me because I'm not like you. Well, guess what? I'll never be like you.'

The Maestro's hands wrap into his shirt, shaking so hard, so hard, so hard. 'You will.' Her voice is a hiss.

'I hate music,' he says, soft as heartbreak and goodbyes and a thousand kilometres beneath the quiet earth.

And he hates that he doesn't quite mean it. He hates *her* music – he's in love with his own.

He's ready for the next slap, but not how she then falls to her knees in a sob, in a scream, and her hand wraps around a jagged shard of plate. Potato drips off it in a pink cloud.

The crockery cuts into her hands, deep, deep, as she squeezes the plate. Her lips move and it takes him a moment to realise the buzzing in his head drowns out her words.

Her whispers are in German. *If only I had no son*.

A sob chokes Beck's throat. Would she try to kill him? 'Don't. Don't. *Don't*.'

Her eyes fix on the shard, on the blood oozing as it cuts through her flesh and hits bone. She's destroying her hand. She's lost. She's not coming back.

Carefully, his mouth bloody, cheek bruised from the slaps, Beck drops to the floor and crawls towards her. He hesitates. She's on her knees, shoulders heaving, blood dripping steadily to the floor. He touches her arm. She doesn't move. So his hands close around her massive wrist and he pries her fingers open one by one until the shard of plate is free and clatters to the tiles.

'J-J-Joey,' Beck says. 'You have to call an ambulance.'

He's not sure if he could without losing himself.

He grabs a tea towel and wraps it around the Maestro's hands. She lets him. She's so blank, so terrifyingly blank. Where is his mother? Beck's eyes blur.

Her lips part, terrified. '*Nein*. No one can see this.'

Everyone should see this.

'You need stitches,' he says.

Why? Why not just leave her on the floor and let her bleed?

Slowly, she's returning – holding the tea towel to her hands herself, straightening, surveying, brain so obviously ticking.

'I can explain this to them.' She licks her lips. 'But not you. Not you.'

Because his face bears the red handprint of her tantrum. They'd call the police.

Does he want that?

'Go.' The Maestro's voice is harsh. 'Go now. I will say I had a fit, I lost my medication. I will *explain this away*.'

Behind him, he hears Joey on the phone, her voice a trembling squeak. 'My mama is hurt and sad. Oh. OK. *Danke*.' She tiptoes over and holds it carefully towards the Maestro.

The Maestro takes it and hangs up. 'They'll still come,' she growls. 'But if you are not here I can do this. I can do this.'

Does he want to be found? Does he? *Does he*?

'Get out.' Her voice rises to a thunderclap. 'Get outside, *Schwachkopf*, or I will tell them you did this to me.' She points a bloodied finger towards Joey. 'And I will do worse to her.'

CHAPTER 15

Why is he so pathetic?

Why?

Cold air touches his bleeding face, soothing like an ice pack. His cheek is swollen, lip broken, and he's cut half a hole in his tongue. It's been worse. One bruise and a bloody mouth is just a warning from the Maestro. Yet it'd be bliss to swallow the winter wind right now and be numb. He wants so badly to be numb.

To forget.

To not think.

He could've stayed – fought for himself, for Joey, told the truth when the ambulance arrived. But the Maestro has always been convincing and he's never had a backbone and he's too scared she'd hurt Joey. *Maybe* if he stayed the truth would come out. *Maybe* the world would pluck him and Joey from their life of piano keys and acidic shouts and hard slaps. *Maybe* he'd lose Joey. Maybe he'd be taken away, far from here, and lose August too.

August.

He runs from his house as the ambulance's red and blue lights appear at the top of the street. He never runs, so it's hard work, but *good*. The ground races away beneath him, dark and uneven, and he stumbles several times, but keeps going. He has no jacket. He has no idea what he should do.

The music in his head has stopped completely. Don't think about that now. Don't *think*.

Linger until the ambulance is gone and then sneak inside? Clean up the Maestro's blood and sweep the smashed dishes and put a Band-Aid over the gangrenous gash in their family?

He's crying. Stupid. He needs to collect himself, not fall into a trembling heap.

Where's he going?

He takes a left down an avenue he's thought about countless times. August's street. What's her number? Nine? No, eleven. And there's a veterinary beside it, or something, or – whatever. He's not going in.

He slows to a jog, legs aching at the stretch of

unused muscles. The houses look sleepy, peaceful, with only the occasional front yard a weedy heap. One house has their garage open, a girl swinging a spanner and plunging her face under a car hood. She looks up as he passes, but he walks faster. Head low. He must look wild.

His body throbs to the beat of the Maestro's metronome slaps. His legs ache from running. The icy night has frozen his split lip. He can't show up on August's doorstep like this. He can't show up at all.

It was his decision to tuck tail between legs and run instead of fighting for help. His decision. *His.*

August does not exist to save him, not when he can *screw his spineless whimpers and save himself.*

He'll just see where she lives. Then he'll go home.

Number eleven Gully Avenue is a squat house with an adjoining veterinary practice in a spruced-up shed. The front yard is crammed with a massive tree, a walled garden and a paved path with pansies in buckets growing around a big sign that reads 'FREY VET AND ANIMAL SHELTER. WE HELP. WE SAVE'.

Beck feels so *stupid* looking at it.

A light glows by the front door, an invitation, a lure. Beck is a moth to it. His feet crunch the sea of buffalo grass and clover as he creeps towards the old Victorian house with its rippled glass door speckled with the warmth of a thousand colours. Faint barking sounds behind the glass, then laughter.

August lives here? Warm and happy and safe?

If he knocks, he'll unleash a legion of pathetic awkwardness. He's never asked for help in his life. He doesn't want it. What does he want?

A family.

An occasional hug.

To know his sister is safe.

A friend.

Something more than a friend?

A safe place to write his music. Which is gone gone gone ... *Don't think about that right now.*

He just wants to talk. That's not pitiful, right? Friend to friend, asking for a second to talk about – anything. Like how dumb his name is, or how he actually adores Twice Burgundy, or how August's crazy healthy food tastes downright delicious no matter how much he mocks it. She'd laugh at him. It'd be normal. He could go home and clean the mess and *breathe*.

His feet betray him and cross the cold wet grass. His hand rises to the door, hesitates. How bad is his face? Is he going to scare her?

Yes.

This is so wrong, so stupid, so needy, so—

He knocks.

Dogs explode into howls and scrabbling paws behind the glass. If August doesn't answer, he'll split because there's no way he's facing her parents with a face like this to ask to see their daughter. But as the seconds tick past, the resolve in his chest caves until he's suffocated with the need to stay.

August answers the door.

She's in red Aztec leggings and a huge cream jumper that comes to her thighs and gapes at the neck. Her fingers barely poke out the ends. Her feet are bare despite her breath frosting as her mouth opens.

'Beck?' Her eyes couldn't get any rounder.

He can smell tomato and rosemary sauce and wine and warmth.

'Who is it, honey?' someone calls.

'My friend from school!' August yells over her shoulder.

She blocks a yapping dog trying to throw itself out the door, which leaves her wedged awkwardly before Beck. 'Shut up, Bo! You too, Gunther.'

With a groan, she gives up and slips fully outside, shutting the front door in the barking faces. She wraps her arms around herself and shivers and Beck feels guilty. Yes. He feels guilty about the *cold air*.

'You're not OK.' It's not a question. 'What happened? Who did this? Can I do something?'

'Petition for world peace?' His nose runs and he has nothing to wipe it with, which is a crippling embarrassment.

August doesn't smile. Beck feels worse.

'I'm s-s-sorry.' His teeth won't stop chattering. 'I shouldn't have—'

'Yes, you should have.' She touches his arm, not quite holding him but somehow pinning him from taking flight. 'This is what friends are for. To help in time of strife and stuff chocolate down your throat when you're miserable. That sort of fun stuff.' Her fingers tighten slightly around his arm. 'You have to come in.'

'No.' He's a knot of panic and horror. 'Your parents – they can't—'

'I'm not letting you freeze on my lawn,' August says. 'You can lie if you want ... and they won't make a fuss. They're totally reasonable folks, trust me.' Her eyes sparkle. 'I'll invent a gloriously distracting reason for your facial features. You wrestle polar bears as an after-school job!'

'Um.'

'You're right. Way too unrealistic. You're a back-alley street fighter.'

'Because that's so much better.'

This is why he came. This is what he needs – a moment under the spell of her smile.

'But seriously,' she says, the joke fading, 'are

you hurt bad? Do you want to call emergency?'

'No.' He doesn't know what he wants. His brain has drowned and he can't make a decision. He can barely breathe.

August nods and yanks the door back open. 'Don't mind the dogs. Most of them won't kill you.'

The heat, the smells, the cheery warbles of happy conversation – he's going to ruin it. He'll wreck August's evening and what if her parents tell the police anyway? His family are the jagged teeth of a saw, but they're all he has and he can't lose that right now.

'I can't, August, I can't—'

But he lets himself be pulled inside.

The dogs hit first, warm and strong, knocking against his legs and leaping all over with wet, rough tongues. Then he's enveloped in warmth, light, the mouthwatering smells of something in the oven. August hauls a few dogs off him and calls uselessly for quiet. She has to pluck one from the chaos, frothing with rage, and shove it in a bedroom with the door shut.

There are animals absolutely everywhere.

He's in a lounge with a hammock full of cats in one corner next to a wall of windows, and the remaining walls are covered in handmade shelves. A woven rug is on the floor and a battered coffee table sports a bonsai tree, a mess of magazines and an unmoving turtle. The ugliest dog Beck's ever seen nestles on a sofa. It looks like something's chewed off its nose and glued it back on.

'That,' August says, noticing his stare, 'is Stuart. Excuse his face. He's been beaten half to death by a disgusting human. We rescued him and while he loves me, he *hates* men. Don't pet him.'

Beck takes a step back as Stuart snarls.

'And this is Tortle.' August picks up the turtle and strokes its shell. 'We didn't know if he was a tortoise or a turtle when we found him, so we covered both bases.'

'Clever,' says Beck.

'Exceptionally.' August sets it back down. 'Plus, with a free-spirited name like Tortle, he won't conform to stereotypes. Look at him now! He's embracing his life with no stereotypical box!'

'Does he own a box?'

'Actually, no.' August beams. 'He's always free. I'm so proud.'

'Question.' Beck squints at the unmoving shell. 'Is it alive?'

'Oh stop it.' She gives his shoulder a gentle, playful nudge. 'You're just jealous of my divergent pet.' She twirls, her gargantuan jumper billowing, and dances down the hallway. 'Hungry?'

'I already ate.' He feels like he's never eaten in his life.

'Does that stop you eating again?' August says.

Unless he wants to stay and get licked by two or nine dogs, Beck has to follow. Every inch of the hallway wall is covered in mismatched photo frames, most starring August pulling faces or cuddling a frog or with green goo mushed over her baby face or her arms draped over her dad's shoulders while she kisses his cheek.

'But first – the bathroom.' August takes Beck's hand and gently pulls him into it. 'Don't even protest. I am excellent at first aid.'

He wants to do more than protest. He wants to run. But he finds himself perching on the edge of a bathtub while August cracks a cupboard door and pulls out a battered first aid kit. This is ridiculous. He's being needy, he—

She rests a hand under his chin and tilts his head upwards. A frown creases her eyebrows. He wishes he wasn't causing that.

'Your cheek isn't too bad,' she says, voice serious, soft. 'Bruising, and a small cut.' She's got a small cloth and she dips it in antiseptic and wipes it across his cheekbone. It stings like fresh hell but he doesn't flinch. He refuses to flinch.

'I can do this myself,' he says.

Her concentrating frown remains. 'I know. But I'm taking care of you for just a hot second, Beck. Let me.'

He does.

Never mind that he can't breathe because her hand is cupped under his chin. Never mind that her skin sets his alight in a way that has nothing to do with stinging cuts.

Please don't stop.

Please don't let go.

Please hold on to me.

She steps back, her brow smoothing. 'Less blood. Still battered.'

She's still holding his hand. He's still letting her.

Her voice drops to a whisper. 'Beck, are you sure I can't—'

'I can handle it. It's not that bad.'

Her smile is very small and very sad. 'Well, I'd better introduce you to my parents before they wonder if we fell down the bathtub plughole.'

She releases his hand and it is a relief – no, no it's not. It is the worst thing.

August leads him to a tiny kitchen, smothered in pot plants and ripe with the juicy odour of lasagne. Music hums softly in the background.

Her dad, an older man than Beck originally guessed from glimpsing him in the car the day August busted her foot, stands at the bench and chops lettuce in an apron proclaiming 'QUEEN OF THE GRILL'. His hair, longer than August's, is looped back with rawhide and the edges of tattoos peek from the collar of his shirt. With a smile, he sets down the knife.

'Hello, hello,' he says, with the kind of voice that would calm an anxious pitbull. 'To whom do I owe this pleasure?' There's a flicker of concern as he looks Beck up and down, and Beck wishes he could dissolve.

'This is Beck,' August says grandly. 'Beck-from-school. You know, the one I gab about all the time.' She winks at Beck. 'Just kidding. I don't talk about you *that* much. He's here for dinner and you absolutely are *not allowed* to ask questions. He wrestles crocodiles.'

Her dad's eyebrows quirk, a gesture Beck knows well from August. And then he just shrugs and keeps chopping lettuce.

'Crocodiles, eh?' her dad says.

'I get into these fights sometimes,' Beck says in a rush. 'It's stupid. I'm stupid.'

Her dad pauses his chopping. 'Really? Doesn't seem like you fought back, son. Did this happen at home?' His voice softens slightly. 'Because I am more than willing to—'

'Those are questions,' August says. 'Please don't scare him off, Dad. *Please*? He's like a delicate, rare flower.'

A woman waltzes into the kitchen then, *literally* waltzes with an imaginary partner. The soft background music is Dvorak – Beck recognises it. Like August's dad, her mother is older, with streaks of grey in honey hair, and she wears fisherman pants and a shirt that looks like it's been woven from moss. When she catches sight of Beck, she pauses the waltz and blinks.

'You look cold, darling,' she says.

Beck has exactly nothing to say.

August says, 'This is Beck and yes, he's cold.'

'I'm fine.' Beck resists rubbing the goosebumps growing up his arms.

'Shane, can't we lend him a jacket?'

'I shall get one directly.' Shane sets down the knife and flips off his apron. He throws it at her. 'Finish the salad, love?'

Her mother takes the apron disdainfully. 'It suits you so much better.'

Shane looks unconcerned. 'It's a salad. What can go wrong? Oh, and we've been expressly forbidden to question August's guest.'

'Not a single question?'

'None.'

'Not even to see if he likes lasagne?'

Shane's eyebrows ask the question – but to August, not Beck, like she's a tunnel one must meet before getting to him.

August considers. Beck is so ashamed and the lump in his throat has bloomed into a small mountain. What kind of family *is* this?

'I'll reword,' she decides. 'No *personal* questions. You're free to inquire about food. And also his favourite colour.'

'Lasagne is great,' Beck says, though he's only ever tasted the packet version. 'But – but I can't stay. I'm sorry. I didn't mean to—'

August's mother picks up the knife and shakes it at Beck. 'We always make far too much lasagne, young man, so I'd be honoured if you'd stay and – oh, August, darling, what have you told him about me? He looks petrified.'

'It's probably the knife you're waving at him,' August says.

Surprised, her mother looks at it and sets it down. 'Oh.'

Shane returns with a lined plaid shirt. He's immensely tall, probably taller than the Maestro's six feet, so Beck nearly disappears into the jacket. But it's warm. It's glorious to be warm. His tongue makes a mangle of the simple *thank you*, but all August's dad says is, 'Call me Shane, and this is Tammy.'

'Careful around my mother,' August whispers, 'or she'll kidnap you and *adopt* you.'

'She does have those tendencies,' Shane says. 'Remember those feral kittens?'

'Do I ever.'

Tammy finishes the salad by dumping in half a jar of olives. 'You must stay, Beck. I insist.'

August pokes Beck's arm and he follows her as she bounces back up the hall. 'Call us,' she says. 'I'm introducing Beck to the house.' She opens a door, also covered in photo frames, and walks in with her arms spread wide. 'My humble abode.' A cat skids between her ankles. 'Careful. The dog bites.'

'More dogs?' Beck says weakly.

A Great Dane sprawls on a battered beanbag in the corner. It growls softly, but judging by the white scales on its eyes, it won't be lunging for him. There's a blue budgie chirping on its head but the Dane doesn't seem to care.

'I think you have more than nine dogs,' Beck says.

'Oh, *I* have nine dogs,' August says. 'My parents also have dogs. Then there's the turtle and an aviary for the birds outside.' She glances at the budgie. 'Most of the birds,' she amends. 'There are a few cats and a goat, but we're only babysitting the llama.'

'Naturally.'

August flops on to her bed. It's covered in handmade quilts and sketchbooks and Sharpies. There are atlas posters on the wall, and her bedside lamp is a repurposed globe. She's not a neat freak, though. There are clothes on the floor and the bin overflows with scraps of half-finished doodles. And the Dane kind of takes up the rest of the space. For all the warmth and cluttered cosiness of the Frey household, it's obvious they're still not well off.

But compared to Beck's sterile room, August's is like a nest of dreams.

August hugs her knees. 'I honestly thought I'd *never* get you to visit. I'm glad you did. Just so you know.'

She looks at him long and hard, so hard that Beck turns away and self-consciously touches his bruised cheek.

'We could talk,' August says.

He can't. Please, don't make him.

But how can he show up and act like a dejected punching bag and not explain?

'It's nothing serious,' he says quietly.

Her eyes say she doesn't believe him. 'I could get ice?'

'The wind kind of iced it on the run over.'

'You ran? Whoa, I didn't think those spindly legs moved that fast.'

He wants to smile, but his cheek hurts.

The joke slips from her voice. 'Is it your mum? You could stay here tonight, if you wanted ...'

'She's in the hospital.'

August's ever-bouncing body freezes, and Beck

realises how it sounds.

'Wait, I didn't – *I* didn't do anything to her.' He says it too fast, too guilty. 'And Joey's with her but she's … she's fine.'

August relaxes back into her cushions. 'OK. That's good, I guess. Are the police involved?'

'No.'

'Should they be?'

'No,' he says dully. 'It's OK. All families have – bumps.' *Or moments when you seriously fear for your life.* 'It's not that bad, really. I'm stupid for coming.'

'Stop saying you're stupid.'

A cat curls around Beck's legs, purring. He's not sure whether to pat it or move away, but the soft, cuddly warmth makes him understand why people like animals.

'This isn't OK, you know.' Her voice is suddenly fierce. 'And it makes me, argh, *so angry* to think of you getting—'

'It's fine.' It's really not. 'Honest, August. I'd do something if it … got too bad.' He wouldn't.

'Dinner!' Tammy hollers from the kitchen.

August sighs. 'Don't freak out now.' She's on her feet, brushing close as she passes. 'I won't let them eat you. We'll just devour lasagne and then I have to show you something spectacular outside before you dash off.'

For once there is no rush. No Maestro at home. No one cares where he is. No one would come looking. But it doesn't feel free. It feels forgotten.

CHAPTER 16

Beck isn't sure how dinner at the Freys' will unfold. Do they pray to a tree? Do they even sit at a table? Is the lasagne actual *real* lasagne? He's never seen August eat meat, so is the lasagne pinned together with dreams of animal freedom and air?

It smells divine, though, and his stomach knots with anticipation. When was the last time he ate food that wasn't cereal?

Turns out the Freys do have a table and they cluster around it like any average family. It's squished in a corner, so wedging another chair in for Beck is an art form. When seated, everyone's elbows nearly touch, and the dishes of food take up so much space, Beck's plate is nearly in his lap.

Tiny hand-painted daisies decorate the plates and the cutlery is mismatched. It's cramped but, somehow, cosy.

'We have a larger table,' Shane says. 'Around here somewhere.' He turns to Tammy, who's slicing an orange into the salad. 'Did we lose the big table?'

'How do you lose a *table*, Dad?' says August.

'Well,' Shane says defensively, 'your mother lost a horse before.'

'It had legs.' Tammy shuffles the huge dish of lasagne, the basket of garlic bread, the salt and pepper shakers, to try and squeeze the salad on to the table.

'Tables have legs,' Shane says.

August helps herself to bread and pesto. 'But they don't run away. That horse ran.'

'She should know,' Tammy agrees. 'She was riding it.'

'Which kind of bothers me –' August reaches for the salad and digs around for oranges and olives '– because you still refer to that escapade as "the time you lost the horse". Not "the time you lost your nine-year-old daughter".'

'But you're like a pigeon, darling. You'd find your way home eventually.' Tammy procures a massive knife from nowhere and cuts the lasagne. It explodes with melting pasta sheets, vegetables and rosemary tomato sauce. Beck keeps his mouth shut in case he drools on his plate.

'Or we could just adopt another child and buy another horse.' Shane passes Tammy his plate. 'Maybe we would've gotten a discount?'

Tammy pauses, red-smeared knife raised disturbingly high. 'Oh, Shane. That's so *true*. Why didn't we think of that instead of chasing them across the state?'

'I think you liked my face,' August says.

She notices Beck isn't moving, so she plucks his plate and passes it to her mother. He *can't* function properly with the smell of food drugging his addled brain. Plus the Freys are terrifying him with banter. They don't seem *real*.

Tammy cuts a massive slice and slaps it on to his plate with a *plop*. 'Presentation isn't my forte,' she says, 'but I didn't make it so it'll definitely taste delicious.'

'That is such a comforting fact.' Shane leans to kiss her cheek.

'Dad,' August says, warningly, 'she's still got a knife.'

'Too true.' He retracts. 'Careful with that, honey. Remember the echidna.'

'Oh, I remember Goliath.'

'I try not to,' August mutters.

Beck decides to let the confusion wash over him and give full attention to the feast on his plate. A quick poke with his fork reveals the lasagne is meatless. But the pasta sheets are gooey with sauce and the vegetables have bathed in a heaven of olive oil and herbs. He can't shovel it in fast enough.

It's easier to think of food than the fact the Freys love each other.

'So,' Shane says, pleasantly. 'No personal questions, I understand. But your favourite colour is an allowable topic, right, Beck?'

'Don't ask about his full name either.' August grins wickedly around the salad dressing at Beck.

Beck would like to stab her right now.

'Um, blue, I guess?' He feels like an idiot. Favourite colour? Are they mocking him or genuinely trying to please August? She's so much like her parents. All the jokes, the unreasonable big words, the quick retorts – she's a carbon copy of her folks.

It scares Beck –

how much he might accidentally resemble

the Maestro.

'Is your full name Beckham?' Tammy says. 'Like the soccer player?'

Beck is saved from answering by a mouthful of pumpkin and lasagne.

'Maybe it's Becktrove,' she says absently, twirling lettuce on her fork.

August groans. 'Mum. Firstly, no one's name is

Becktrove. Where on earth did that even come from? Secondly, I just said it's *not* a good topic.'

'Well what *is* a good topic?' Tammy says.

What about nothing? What about silence, so they can pay the proper homage to the delicious lasagne? He's nearly finished his piece before he realises everyone else has barely gotten through a corner.

'Beck is a musician,' August says.

Beck chokes. This serves him right for never being honest. If she knew about the piano, knew *everything*, then she wouldn't touch the subject. But he can't be honest.

'He's also in love with Twice Burgundy,' August says, 'although, strictly, he's a classical man.'

'I am a classical woman,' Tammy says, holding her fork over her heart. 'Do you like Bach? Chopin? Beethoven?'

August gives him a conspiratorial kick under the table and he whacks her right back. She yelps and then smothers her laughter with a huge forkful of lasagne. This girl is maddening.

Beck's mouth is dry. 'I like Grieg.'

'Grieg!' Tammy pokes her husband – with her fork, no less – and grins at him. 'Most teenagers don't even know who Bach is, let alone *Grieg*! He knows things, Shane, this one *knows things*.'

'That was pointed,' Shane says.

'Yes, dear, it's a fork.'

'No, I mean the comment.' He frowns at her over his half-full wine glass. 'I was nineteen when we met and, fine, I *didn't* know who Bach was. I thought you liked dogs. That's why I kept hanging out with you. *I* liked dogs. You liked Bach, or whatever. We got married and I realised my mistake.'

'You were both studying to be vets, Dad,' August says. 'The mistake was pretty acceptable.'

'Thank you.' Shane cuts his lasagne majestically. 'See? That is why we traipsed across the state to find you, instead of adopting another child. We like how positive and encouraging you are.'

Tammy pops out of her chair. 'Let me dish you up some more, Beck.'

He tries to say *no thanks*, to be polite, because he's pretty sure he could polish off the dish, but his plate is already piled high.

'Yes, feed him up,' August says. 'He gets super cranky when he's hungry – I survived an attack once.'

'You're seriously mean to me,' Beck says.

'That's why you like me.'

No, he likes her because there's sunshine in her eyes and she knows the secrets to smiling.

Beck sets to work on his second piece and doesn't answer.

'Now, Beck,' Shane says seriously. 'I would just like to extend the invitation of dinner here, whenever you need it. I would also like to, well, if we could have a little talk before you go about your, ah, face and—'

'I'm fine,' Beck says. 'This was just a stupid misunderstanding with some … *guys*.' Could he be a more unconvincing liar? 'I am really sorry for disrupting—'

Something in Shane's eyes say he doesn't buy it, but he merely holds up a hand and says, 'Do not be. I refuse to hear apologies for gracing our fine home with your waif-like presence.'

'Dad,' August says, 'that's not very nice.'

'Well, he reminds me a little of Oliver Twist,' Shane protests. 'Plus it's nice to see some of August's friends once in a while. She never brings them around.'

August starts clearing plates. 'Because they're all terrified of you. And your food. And our dogs.'

Beck stumbles to help her, although stacking other people's plates comes with a mountain of pressure. He doesn't want to be all *thanks-for-the-meal-and-here-let-me-accidentally-drop-and-smash-all-your-crockery*. So he goes for the plastic salad bowl and gingerly takes it to the kitchen. August laughs silently.

'Why are they terrified of me?' Shane looks

alarmed. 'If you're referring to the time of Andrea and the python—'

August shudders. 'Don't rehash that story. Andrea doesn't even *talk* to me any more, by the way. You scarred her for *life*.'

'What about Sumi and Ajeet?'

Her nose wrinkles. 'They're busy, OK? At least I *have* friends. Beck over here is a moody hermit.'

'Please, no,' Beck whispers.

'He has exactly one friend,' August goes on.

'Who?' her father says.

She glares.

'Oh. *Oh* yes. You.'

'I'm glad you came to that conclusion so fast.' She clears his plate while he's still taking a last bite of garlic bread.

He huffs and feeds the crust to one of the many dogs sniffing under the table. A cat has climbed on to Beck's vacated chair and mews piteously.

'I have cashew ice cream for dessert,' Tammy says. 'And fresh cherries.'

'Cherries aren't in season, darling,' Shane says.

'Then un-fresh cherries.' Tammy looks like she's considering standing, but not sure if the effort is worth it.

Beck understands. He's absolutely *stuffed*. And he hasn't felt that way in – ever? Cashew ice cream sounds dubious at any rate, so as he gives August a pleading look and she understands.

'Actually, I'm liable to pop,' August says. 'Can we skip? I need to show Beck outside before he goes.'

'But it's dark,' her mother says.

'That is quite perfect for what I want to show him.'

Shane shares a mock aghast look with his wife and then slams a hand on the table. Three dogs skid out from under it. 'Now, young lady, there will be no—'

August covers her face. '*Please* don't say anything embarrassing to me, Dad. I beg you. I'm showing him the *stars*. The stars in the sky that *God has made*. If you embarrass my friend to death I swear I will run away from home and live in Paraguay.'

Tammy sighs. 'Paraguay is such a long way off, Shane, darling. Leave the poor children be. Beck looks a little shell-shocked by us as it is.' She waves them off. 'Off you go. Stargaze. Freeze your appendages off.'

August beams like a child with chocolate, and then tugs Beck out the back door.

'No hanky panky!' her dad calls.

'Darling,' Tammy says, 'no one says that any more.'

The back door claps shut and the Frey parents

are silenced. The night wraps cool, sweet arms around Beck's throbbing head.

He follows August down a pebble path. 'Your family is …'

'Intense. I *know*. But they only mean to squish you with love and weirdness and puppies. Some people are suited to non-judgemental animal company, don't you think?'

'Actually, I was going to say they're nice.'

She quiets. Beck feels guilty, like he's playing the *woe is me* card since the reason he's here is because his mother is nothing like hers. Gingerly, she slips her hand into his. His heart leaps.

'Come with me,' she whispers.

Beck is endlessly glad for the borrowed jacket, although the blush creeping up his neck warms him too. She's *holding his hand again*. What's he supposed to do with this feeling?

Solar lights mark the way down the pebble path, circuiting several old, swooping trees. They pass two kennels and a dog starts howling.

'That's Caligula.' August moves fast to bypass the hysterical animal. 'He'd probably kill you. He'd probably kill *me*. Manners aren't his strong point.'

'So you save all these animals just … just because?' All Beck can think of is the Maestro telling him how he's just a project to August. He's a number out of a hundred on the list of things she's 'saved'. How is he supposed to ignore that, to think he's more than a pitiful reject in her eyes?

August shrugs. 'Yes? Sort of? We try to get them adopted out too. We run newspaper ads and give out flyers and convince everyone we meet how much they need a psychotic, not-house-trained, abused, partially blind labradoodle in their lives.'

'How often does it work?'

'Relatively well. I'm very convincing.'

That's true.

The backyard is damp with night tears. Gardens are barricaded with mossy logs and rocks, and staghorns droop from the huge trees. Beck breathes grass clippings and orchids and starlight.

August takes him to a hammock. It's the flat kind, wide as a mesh bed that at least five people could lie on while gazing up through the trees at the sky. She flops on to it and, even though Beck protests, she grabs the corner of his jacket and tugs him down.

They're very close. Arm wedged against arm. His hand brushes hers and her hair tickles his ears. He's terrified of how comfortable this is, of how close and warm and safe he feels.

He's not a fool. Blink and this is over. He'll go back to his piano, the Maestro, the agony, because as much as he hates it, it's all the family he has.

But right now? He has a second of August and stars and magic.

'Behold,' August says. 'The most beautiful sight in existence.'

Their feet trail the grass as they both rock the hammock gently and watch the map of stars above. He's never paid attention to anything but music before. Semiquavers and chromatic scales, Liszt and Rachmaninoff and Chopin. Music he's forced to play and music he could compose. They are his language, his focus, his life. He's never looked at the stars before, never realised they're freakishly entrancing.

And slowly, one note at a time, the music in his head begins again – soft and scared – but *there*. It terrifies him, the thought that one day the Maestro might hit him enough for his music to disappear for ever.

He taps a rhythm on his thigh to see if the notes will disappear again.

They stay. Twirling under his skin.

'I did write something for you.' It just comes out, and part of Beck feels stupid, the other part brave.

'Really?' August nestles her head next to his. 'Can I hear it?'

'It's awful.'

'I know it's not.'

'You've never heard me play.'

She snorts, which sort of breaks the electric brilliance of the sky and the stars and the quietness. Beck relaxes into the hammock with a half smile.

'You think you're a mystery,' she says, 'but I've figured out a lot. I'm a sleuth like that.'

'Oh really?'

'Yes. I know you breathe music, but it embarrasses you and maybe you even hate it a little. Which is confusing,' she adds. 'I know your home sucks—' She cuts off his mumbled protest. 'But despite that, you're a marshmallow *and* a fantastic big brother, because Joey is proof of that.'

'You mean the kid who's been suspended from preschool?'

'Joey is incredible.' August gives the hammock an energised push. 'I also know what you dream of.'

How much does she think about him?

As much as he thinks about her?

'Escape,' she says, like she's plucked the word from between the rusty piano strings that bind his heart together.

He feels hollow without his secret.

'But,' she says, slowly, 'you're trapped.'

He wants to tell her about Germany – about staying or going. Not that it's his choice, it never will be, but no matter which direction the Maestro binds him to, it'll be the wrong one. Leaving Joey? Leaving August? Unthinkable. Staying? He's going to snap someday.

'You like me because I'm pathetic,' he says suddenly. 'Like your dogs.'

He wishes he could take it back. Did he just splinter their night with his poisoned self-loathing?

'You're not as cute as my dogs,' she says.

He should've known she couldn't take anything seriously. It stabs him, a little, because he can't joke all the time. He should go, unravel and collapse somewhere in private.

'Although, for the record,' she says, stern now, the joke vanished, 'you're not pathetic. Why do you even think that? You're actually funny and protective and kind. You could've let me limp home when I was an idiot and busted my foot. Did you? Nope. And even though Joey stands there swearing like a trooper, I've *never* heard you get riled up. Like I said, you're a marshmallow with burnt skin, but I see you, Beck.'

She hooks her fingers through his, fast, like she thinks he's going to make a break for it. His fingers close around hers – it's not awkward, it never could be.

'You're not a puppy to be rescued,' she says softly. 'You're a boy I frequently feel intensely about.'

'Intensely?'

'It's very distracting,' August adds. She lets out a small giggle.

'What?' Beck says.

'I'm just thinking of your reaction.'

'To what?'

She pushes herself up on her elbow. 'To this.' And she kisses him, very gently, very cautiously, on his broken lip.

CHAPTER 17

The Maestro smells of hospital and cinnamon tea. She huddles in bed, her ancient laptop groaning as she emails music theory corrections to her students at the university. Beck has a spatula in his hand, still coated in batter from the pancakes he's making Joey for dinner.

She called him and he came. He's obedient like that.

It's been three days since her outrage, since his beating, since August's kiss. The Maestro hasn't really left her bed and hasn't spoken to him, no apology, of course, and no explanation for what happened at the hospital. Clearly they swallowed whatever lie she concocted. Beck's decided not to care. He *doesn't care*.

'Shut the door,' the Maestro says.

Beck looks at her heavily bandaged hands that struggle to keep a mug of tea upright.

'I want it open.' Beck leans against the doorframe and folds his arms, spatula in the crook of his elbow. 'I have the pan on. For Joey's dinner, considering you don't cook for her.'

The Maestro's lips thin. 'Your attitude is unacceptable.'

Beck shrugs. Bruises still linger on his face. Her artwork.

'But,' the Maestro says, 'you are under pressure, *Junge*. I see that.'

'I don't want to play for my uncle.'

The Maestro leans back in her pillows. 'I did not ask if you *wanted* to. You will.' Her tone goes crisp. 'But it would be a miracle if your uncle saw potential in you, so do not fret over moving to *Deutschland* any time soon.'

Is it relief or a slap? Beck can't even sort through the jumble of his pain to figure it out.

'But you will still play,' she says. 'And as rude as you are, *Sohn*, I will reward you for a good performance.'

This is surprising. Although her idea of a 'reward' is probably more scales.

'That girl,' the Maestro begins, and Beck's heart

thuds. 'That party. You may go.'

'Really?' It pops out, desperate and unbelieving, before Beck can be cautious.

'*Ja.*' The Maestro's lips twist, sour at his excitement. 'Mayhap this will encourage you to work harder before the concert. Hard work might even cover up your lack of talent.'

Beck has to keep the Maestro happy – or at least not bitterly disgusted with him – if he wants to be allowed the party privilege.

He glues himself to the piano, practising so long and hard he gets a headache from his own cacophony. The Maestro gradually resumes her motivational insults, but keeps her hands off. This could be because they're still bandaged. Or she's sorry she lost control so badly that night?

Who is Beck kidding? She could never be sorry.

And in between the Chopin, Beck composes for August.

It's coming along nicely.

While Chopin is precise notes, fast and light and powerful, his song for August is the opposite. It's slow and filled with pauses of regret and rushes of longing and the occasional dance. It tastes like thunderstorms when he dreams of it at night.

But he honestly does focus on the Chopin, because he wants it to be right. For his uncle, for the Maestro. For himself. He doesn't want to be embarrassed. And a stupid, deluded part of his soul still claws with whispers of *maybe she'll approve of your playing, claim you as her talented son, and spontaneously combust into loving you.*

Yeah, and maybe the world will end.

He doesn't need the Maestro's approval. What he needs is a way to give August her song for her birthday – which is the same day as his private lesson with Jan Keverich.

He's so busy composing and practising and actively *not thinking* about August's kiss that the day of his uncle's recital creeps up and slaps him in the face.

They're all going. The Maestro has her bandages off. Joey has a too-small pink dress, which, coupled with a bow in her wild hair, makes her look ridiculous.

She slinks into his room with her gumboots sticking out from the skirt and the bow already crumpled. She hasn't quite regained her bounce since the Maestro struck her, a fact that gnaws at Beck.

'Do I look like Beauty and the Best?' Joey says.

'Actually, it's *beast*.' Beck is mostly dressed, ignoring nervous pangs. Last time he readied for a concert it ended with getting beaten bloody near a bus stop.

Joey stares at the piano and then, cautiously, taps at a few keys. How can she even look at the piano now? Or does she not remember the Maestro's threats for her to start? It hasn't been mentioned since and her five-year-old brain probably has dismissed it. If only Beck had the same faith.

He buttons his shirt – and realises something's wrong. The suit jacket strains a little over his chest, but it's the *sleeves*. He checks his trousers. There's a fair amount of ankle showing.

No, no, *no*.

He grew?

He can't have grown that much.

No.

He can't turn up at some concert for rich people, to impress his uncle, to prove his worth to the Maestro *wearing this*. And they are leaving in less than an hour. His hands tremble as he tugs at his trouser legs, imagining the Maestro's oncoming rage. She can't blame him for growing ... OK, she probably will. *Please, please, stretch*. Does he have the worst luck in the universe?

Joey giggles. 'Beck, you growed! Mama!' she yells. 'Beck doesn't fit his clothes!'

The Maestro appears with her hair worryingly flat – how violently did she beat it into submission? – and wearing a gown from her glory days. She had everything custom made since she was once rich, famous *and* an unusual size. She looks fierce, proud, even beautiful, a pianist to be in awe of.

Beck looks like a nitwit.

Joey points, like the Maestro might not see the problem. 'He's gonna split his *pants*.'

Beck gives her a filthy glare, but truth is – he might.

'This is my fault,' the Maestro says.

Beck gapes. Isn't it his fault for not asking permission to shoot up several centimetres?

'I never thought of your suit,' she says. '*Verdammt*.'

'You're a giraffe,' Joey adds, helpfully.

'I know.' Beck grinds his teeth. Unless he wants to appear in one of the Maestro's dresses, this is it. Hello circus act.

The Maestro is silent for a long time, long enough for Beck's panic to flip up a notch. Then, her lips pursed, she says, 'Put on tall black socks.'

Beck lunges for his wardrobe and digs out socks. He can't wear his trousers low and still be able to tuck in his shirt, so the socks are the only solution. At least his suit jacket doesn't let him down *too* badly, and if he doesn't reach for anything he should be fine.

'You'll do,' the Maestro says. 'And *beeile dich*! Being late is unacceptable.'

They take the bus, dressed in their finery, and ignore the stares.

217

Beck doesn't bring sheet music.

The last stretch of the journey must be taken in a taxi, where the Maestro grinds her teeth and Beck winces at the exorbitant price. Apparently buses don't go into the *rich* part of the city. Here, you should have a car. And probably a maid and a gardener and a cook. *Meine Güte*, the houses are huge! Beck plasters his face against the window as the taxi purrs past manicured lawns and circular driveways, fountains and huge gates with wrought iron symbols.

It's like a picture book where the princess is going to a ball.

Except Beck is no princess, rather a giraffe waltzing towards certain doom. Yes, he has exactly zero confidence in himself by this point. He just hopes the Maestro leaves him alive afterwards.

The taxi deposits them at the end of the white stone driveway, and they walk up in awe. There are cars everywhere, expensive cars, and their polished sides reflect Beck's face as he passes. The lawn is a sea of green and there are actually *butlers* at the door. They welcome, direct, nod politely. The Maestro holds tight to Joey in case she makes a break for it to paddle in the goldfish pond by the front door.

One of the attendants takes their names and, on hearing the name Keverich, leads them in himself.

Beck thinks he sees a raised eyebrow, but can he blame the guy? Joey is still wearing gumboots. Beck's suit doesn't fit. The Maestro is too tall, too broad, to be an average mortal. They are ridiculous.

'The recital will be in the ballroom,' the attendant says.

The ballroom. Of course. Is the food being served on golden plates, too?

They pass white-carpeted staircases and gold-trimmed rugs, and then enter the ballroom. There must be a hundred people in here, dressed for an opera, their conversation a level murmur. Floor-length windows open on to a deck and Beck can smell food. Oh, *food*. Then he looks for the piano.

It sits at the far end of the room, surrounded by white cushioned chairs, and polished to a blinding sheen. Is he terrified to play it? Or longing?

The room, the house, the air, all stink of money.

Joey spies the food laid out on the verandah – cocktail meats, chocolates and miniature cucumber sandwiches.

'I'm starved,' Joey declares.

'So am I,' he whispers. 'But you have to be *quiet* about this.'

'So I gotta quietly eat everything?'

'Um. Try to avoid stuffing your face at least?'

Joey wiggles her hand out of the Maestro's – which is surprisingly easy since the Maestro has been enveloped by a swarm of socialites. It's like a curtain falls off her face and the Maestro is gone, replaced with someone whose body language is soft and welcoming, whose lips twist into the right words and let out the correct volume of laughter.

She fits here. This is where she came from.

It makes Beck wonder how much money she used to have back in Germany – and if she misses it.

He's left to trail after Joey.

It's not time to freak out yet anyway, is it? For all he knows Jan Keverich is watching him – but he's never met his uncle, never seen a photo. And making sure his sister doesn't impale herself on a toothpick is more important. Nervous breakdowns can come later.

The air is cooler outside and it smells of citrus oil and eucalyptus leaves. There are significantly fewer people out here – weird, because this is where the food is. A few waiters carry silver trays of crackers with salmon pâté, slivers of cheesecake and asparagus wrapped in silverside.

Joey prowls along the length of the table, her nose wrinkled. She finds a plate with toothpicks of cocktail sausages, sharp cheese and pickled onions and takes two.

'What are the white balls?'

'Pickled onions,' Beck says. 'You'll love them.'

Joey sucks the onion off the end. Her lips pucker. Then her eyes bulge as the acidic juice attacks her throat and Beck nearly dies holding in his laughter. He's so mean. But he couldn't resist. He turns away, faking a sneeze, as a waiter appears with a tray of fudge brownies in meticulous triangles.

The waiter presents the tray. '*Guten Tag*,' he says. 'Good afternoon.' His German accent is perfect.

Beck smiles politely. Joey chokes.

The waiter looks mildly concerned. 'Is she quite all right? Some water, maybe?'

'She's experiencing a pickled onion for the first time.' Beck eyes the brownies with their dollar-sized squirt of cream on top.

Joey gives a hacking cough and then swipes a brownie off the tray. Overcome with onion, she still can't speak, but Beck guesses she'll live if she's planning for the future with brownies.

The waiter laughs.

'She really likes chocolate,' Beck explains. *She never gets it at home.*

'Chocolate is a substance worth existing for,' says the waiter.

Joey, finally getting her breath back, turns around and kicks Beck in the shins.

He yelps. 'Joey,' he hisses. 'Not *here*.' He glances, embarrassed, at the waiter as if to say *little kids*, *what can you do?* But the waiter laughs far too hard.

'You could've told me it was spicy!' Joey shouts.

Heads turn.

Beck deserves it, but it's still embarrassing. 'Sorry? It's not actually spice—'

'I could've died.' Joey takes a vicious bite of the brownie. 'And then I wouldn't get to hear Uncle Jan play the piano so much better than you.'

The waiter slides his tray of brownies back on the table. 'How do you know your brother is not better than your uncle?'

Joey has a smudge of cream on her nose. 'Because Mama says Beck is bad.'

Beck stops regretting the onion surprise. His collar feels too tight, and he reminds himself Joey's only parroting and doesn't really understand. Except ... what if the Maestro isn't hiding her true feelings to other people either? What if he sits down to play and they all laugh?

The waiter has to wipe his eyes from laughing so hard. 'Why didn't Ida tell me how priceless you two are?'

Oh.

No?

'Um, Uncle ... Jan?' Beck says like the complete idiot he is.

'*Ja*,' his uncle says. 'I meant to introduce myself whilst offering you food, because I hear that is how one wins favour with small children, but it escaped me as I watched Johanna encounter pickled onions.'

Joey puts a hand – unfortunately tainted with chocolate and cream – on her hip. 'Are you tricking us?'

'Joey,' Beck hisses.

Jan shakes his head, sorrowful. 'I did trick you, little Johanna. Allow me to make it up to you with a small gift of chocolate.' He pulls three small chocolate bars, wrapped in gold foil, from his pocket.

Her eyes narrowed, she takes one. Then she takes a second. 'This is for Mama,' she says, and Beck knows there's exactly no possibility the Maestro will receive one of those chocolates.

'You are so sweet,' says Jan, smiling.

Joey swipes the third and runs off.

Jan straightens, still chuckling softly. 'Ah, children. They are so delightful.'

They are when you give them chocolate.

'You two make me regret marrying my music and never having children,' Jan says.

Beck says nothing. He's not sure *what* to do now. This is Jan Keverich, the famed pianist, the estranged and childless uncle, the rich possible benefactor. Everything the Maestro said made Beck think Jan would be as terrifying as her. He's built the same – tall, broad, with long slim fingers and the trademark Keverich pepper curls. But he's butter in Joey's paws.

How is he *brother* to the Maestro?

Jan smooths his jacket and does up a single button. His suit fits like he was born for it, and staring at it just makes Beck tug harder at his sleeves.

'I have wanted to meet you for years, Beethoven.'

'I go by Beck,' he says. 'If that's OK.'

Jan smiles. 'I don't blame you. Musician names are the Keverich curse. Still –' his long fingers knit together '– great names beget *wunderbare* pianists.'

'I wouldn't know,' Beck says.

'I do not believe your sister,' Jan says with a wink. 'I have utmost faith in your playing, Beck. I also look forward to our private time tomorrow to discuss music without audience. Music is more relaxing without expectations.' He indicates the ballroom with a polite sweep of the hand. 'Shall we return?'

Time to begin the torture? But Beck is strangely heartened that Jan prefers to play alone too.

'You feel – um, judged – when you play?' Beck follows him between rows of paintings.

'Absolutely,' Jan says. 'I often lose myself in a piece, but other times? *Keine Beziehung.*' *No connection.* His tone is factual. 'Often an inexperienced audience cannot tell. Let us hope, though, that you and I both feel the music this evening. Passion is more important than perfection.'

Has the Maestro heard that? She needs to.

Half the guests are seated when they arrive before the monstrous piano. People still chat and mingle with glasses of champagne until a man with the physique of a bowling ball instructs all to find seats.

'That is our host,' Jan says quietly, 'Audwin Denzel. He is a good friend of mine and in awe of our work.'

Our work. Jan is in for a headache of embarrassment when Beck pounds the piano keys. The audience blurs a little before Beck, lost in sweat and nerves. If he stares too hard at the piano, he can see his own petrified face.

The Maestro sits in the front row. Joey, smeared with chocolate and busily playing with her three empty wrappers, is sprawled on the floor beside her.

Jan approaches her and she rises, her face impassive.

'Ida,' Jan says. 'I have met your son.'

How can he be so cheerful? How can he not flinch at the stone and ice in her eyes?

'I need a word with him before you begin,' the Maestro says.

Jan nods, '*Ja*. Of course. We will start when you are ready, Beck.'

He crouches to talk to Joey as the Maestro strides a few paces from them. Beck has nothing to do but follow. Behind him, Joey garbles, 'I wuv chothlate,' with a sticky mouthful.

In front of him, the Maestro whispers in ice.

'You are to play first,' she says, 'and then next is your uncle and the true performance of this evening. I refuse to be embarrassed by you, *Junge*, do you hear me? I know this piece is inside you.' She jabs a finger at his skull. 'There will be consequences if you fail and you will pay. Whatever it takes. I will *not* be made a fool.'

Pay. Consequences.

Pain.

Beck says, 'I'll do my best.'

'No.' The Maestro wraps her useless fingers around his arm and draws him close, close, so the ice falls down his neck and his lungs fill with glaciers. 'You will do *better*, or ...' Her voice hardens. 'Or I will *break your hands*.'

Beck jerks away, the glacier splintering, stabbing his heart.

Would she? Is it a threat of desperation and fury?

Or

would

she?

Beck tucks his hands behind his back.

'Go play.' The Maestro gives a dismissive wave.

He takes himself to the piano. She would do it. She *would*.

How could he let her?

How could he stop her?

Beck stands beside Jan without realising he got there. The crowd hushes and several lights dim.

Jan raises a hand for silence and then, in the hush, he says, '*Willkommen!* Ladies and gentlemen, friends and associates and, of course, *willkommen* to the guests of honour – my dear sister, my niece and finally my nephew, who will play for us this evening.'

There's a gentle wave of applause. They swim before him, like his icy insides are melting and he's being forced to swim. His head is gone, gone, *gone*.

The clapping subsides and Jan continues. 'My nephew, named after the famous Beethoven –' his German accent caresses the well-known name '– will be performing two études for us this evening. Then I have a concerto to share with you, my friends. My nephew is a prodigy of the piano and considers returning to Germany to study from the greats.'

Applause again.

Beck didn't know he was *considering*. He thought he was either being picked or dismissed. He wonders if, perhaps, the Maestro hasn't been relaying what Jan says.

'I do thank you,' Jan says, 'for honouring me with your presence on my brief Australian tour. Many thanks to our host, Audwin Denzel, for providing his home for this musical rendition.' He leans towards Beck and whispers, 'Would you like to announce your piece?'

Beck seems to have lost his wits. He'll probably find them at some point. But right now, he's blinking furiously as the crowd transforms into a sea of sharks with hungry eyes. He forces his brain to the Chopin. Remember it, *remember it*. The Maestro won't let him live past a second bout of stage fright. He knows those études, the notes are burned to his bones.

He'll do this, he *can* do it. He's not going to fail. He takes a deep breath.

And then he sees her.

Why – what –

how is she here?

Her dress is a wispy green, her feet confusingly shod in silver high heels, and her hair is braided with silver ribbons. She looks comfortable, excited, sitting beside her parents, and her eyes are only for him.

August burns with admiration.

She can't be here. This isn't the place for her. She belongs in the stars with a turtle on her lap and Twice Burgundy in her ears. Not *here*. If she sees him, she'll know.

She'll know how much he hates music. How scared of it he is. How it controls his life.

Vaguely, he's aware of Jan announcing the Chopin études in the wake of Beck's silence, and then, with a gentle but firm push, he sends Beck towards the piano. August is gone from his vision. He only sees the rows of piano teeth and wonders if they'll devour him.

Jan's voice is in his ear. 'Are you all right?'

He has to be. He has no choice.

He has to play perfectly.

As answer, he slips on to the cushioned stool and his fingers glide across the keys. How can something so terrifying be so beautiful?

How can his future depend on seven minutes on the piano?

Why couldn't he be more than this?

He has to stop thinking of the Maestro's threats. Think of something else. Think of – August. He imagines the hammock, the galaxies painted like glitter across the black sky above, her kiss that stole his heartbeat.

Beck's fingers tremble into the keys for the first

few bars – and then he plays the fire and wild dancing passion of Chopin.

He plays perfectly.

CHAPTER 18

Except for one note.

CHAPTER 19

For seven suffocating minutes, Beck plays those études. Notes tangle at a thousand kilometres an hour, complicated, exact, powerful. Those minutes crack his ribcage and pry music out of his soul like his life depends on it.

And then –

fumble.

He launches for the finale, for the chord that will linger across the room – but when his fingers land, it's *wrong*.

Dissonant. One incorrect note and his world falls to ashes.

Beck snaps his hands away, panicked, hot with terror. *Howcouldhedothat?* He's never made that mistake before. Does he replay the ending? Does he try again for the last chord? But he can't – a professional musician ignores his mistakes.

But –

no.

His shoulders hunch.

He nearly doesn't notice the cascade of applause behind him, and it takes him a second to remember to stand, to bow. His face is beetroot. How can they even clap for *that*? He looks for August, but the mass of faces blur and he feels dizzy with the effort of staying on earth.

But he can see the Maestro just fine.

Joey stands on a chair and claps furiously, pausing to whoop, which is as flattering as it is embarrassing.

And the Maestro? She doesn't clap. For once her hands don't even shake as she curls them into fists. Her eyes shine with furious tears.

How dare she cry.

Beck moves away from the piano. He feels like he just swam through a frozen river and each step is a sluggish effort. He wants to throw up. Or combust. He takes the seat beside Joey and waits for his heartbeat to calm, for his senses to return. He's dimly aware of more music as Jan begins to play – light and cheeky at first, and then cascading down into a waterfall of swift, passionate

233

notes. Beck can't focus. He doesn't even react when Joey whispers, far too loudly, in his ear, 'You're my bestest brother,' and gives him a chocolate-smeared hug.

He just stares at his hands.

Even when it's over, when Jan has finished his thirty-minute concerto and the crowd is milling once more, Beck is still rooted in his stupor. He smiles at blurred faces and repeats the name of his piece half a million times. He knows his palms are sweaty, his trousers ridiculously short, and his attention gone – but what they think no longer seems important. Not with the reality of the Maestro's threats crushing his lungs.

He knows what is coming.

Then Jan rescues him, taking over conversations while spouting ridiculous sentences in German of *how talented is my nephew!* and *unbelievable genius* while Beck exits.

But wrong note

wrong note

wrong note.

'You look pale. Let me get you some water,' Jan says and disappears.

Beck wishes he could melt into the wall. But the Maestro? Who knows where she's gone? Should he find her, or run away, or explain to Jan or—

August is in front of him.

She looks amazing and sophisticated but still carefree and slightly impish. Up close he can see the bodice of her gown is a beaded gecko. She has a fishnet cardigan on because, as always, she rejects the notion that it's autumn. And shoes? He's barely seen her in runners let alone *heels*.

'You liar.' She gives his shoulder a gentle shove. 'You said you weren't "that good".'

'I'm not.'

'Ugh, Beck.' She groans and tips back her head, as if imploring the universe to give her strength to put up with this idiot. 'You are a freaking piano wizard. I've never seen anyone play that – that fast, and good, and *amazing*. How many times am I allowed to say amazing? Because you are amazing.'

'You've definitely reached your limit.'

'You were *inside* the piano.' August's breath catches. 'I've never seen anyone so into music like that. It was –' she leans forward and whispers '– *amazing*.'

This is everything he's ever wanted to hear. So why does he want to cry?

He blinks furiously and stares past her, focusing on anything, everything, but August. 'Why are you here?'

August waves behind her. 'My parents. Mum is nuts about classical music, but she's been mispronouncing your last name all week and I had no idea.' She leans close, her eyes widening. 'And your uncle is incredible. I mean, you're good and definitely much cuter, but his fingers were doing all these crazy—' She breaks off with a laugh. 'Well, duh. You know. You're basically a piano yourself.'

She shouldn't be here.

It wouldn't be as bad if she wasn't here.

'Beck?' August touches his arm so very lightly. 'What's wrong? Hey, hey – it's OK.'

Great. So now he looks like he's going to cry? Of all the unfairness.

'Did something happen?' August's voice lowers. 'Are you hurt?'

'No.' It's a staccato sob.

Pull yourself together, you *Schwachkopf*.

'You need some air.'

She kidnaps him from the ballroom, from the piano, from the chatter and chaos. The air on the verandah is cool and tinged with dusk. Joey is, predictably, prowling the table again, this time munching spring rolls and mint wafers and avoiding pickled onions.

He leans against the balcony, staring into a backyard of perfect grass, crystal-clear swimming pool and rows of box-shaped hedges. August hangs next to him, shivering slightly in the evening coolness. The cool air is good. He's calmer. He's not going to cry.

236

'How do you not see how good you are?' August says.

He doesn't answer.

August shifts closer so their shoulders touch. 'You're pretty wickedly talented, Keverich. I'll even risk saying I like your music better than Twice Burgundy and you *know* how much I'm sacrificing to say that. I'll have to cancel my wedding to both of them—'

He grabs her arm, turns her to face him – too rough, too fast, but he seems to have lost all fine motor control. She tilts her head, surprised.

'August,' he says. 'I-I-I hate it. I hate music. I don't want to do this.'

Her lips part, but she can't form the question.

He lets go of her and steps back. How *dare* he be rough. 'I'm sorry. I'm – I'm sorry.'

'It's OK,' she says, but he's not sure it reaches her eyes.

There's a clatter behind them and they both jump. Joey has dragged a chair over to the table so she can sit properly and devour the cheese platter.

Beck focuses on the balcony rail. 'I'm coming to your party tomorrow.'

'Really?' she says. 'That's awesome, that's – unexpected, actually.'

He starts to say, 'If I'm still invited ...'

But she groans. 'Yes, you are, you dork. You're

the moodiest person I know, of course, and totally *boring*, but I think I'll find it in my heart to be excited for a freaking piano genius at my party. But you have to bring a present.' She pauses, considering. 'An enormous one. It's the entry fee.'

If he wrote out her song, would it be enough?

'Is that enormous as in weight or height?'

'Height.' She stands on tiptoes and kisses his cheek. 'Stop growing. We used to be compatible and now I have to wear heels. You could probably get some new trousers though.'

'How bad is it? Honestly?'

'Borderline hilarious, but we won't dare laugh because somehow you make it cute.'

'Lucky me.'

August's smile is sad. 'Lucky you.'

The Keverichs are the last to leave.

Joey's collapsed in a food coma on the floor and Beck isn't sure whether he's starving or wants to puke. It's near midnight and he doesn't want to be alone with the Maestro.

Jan offers to carry Joey out to the waiting taxi. She has chocolate-smudged cheeks and greasy handprints over her dress and she fits in Jan's arms perfectly.

The walk to the car is quiet. The Maestro seems to have nothing to say to her estranged brother and Beck is just enjoying his last minutes in safety. When Jan leaves ...

Stop it. Don't think like that. The Maestro's not going to—

'I'll see you tomorrow, Beck,' Jan says. 'Bright and early, *ja*?'

'*Ja*,' Beck says, on automatic.

'I am not in the country long,' Jan says. 'Mayhap I could take you and the children out, Ida? Dinner?'

The Maestro doesn't slow. 'I am sure you have much more important things to do.'

This confuses Beck. Sure, the Maestro is furious, but at *Beck*, not Jan. Doesn't she want to butter him up so he'll take Beck to Germany?

Apparently Jan is immune to her coldness. 'Nothing more important than the family I have neglected to connect with for over a decade.'

They reach the taxi and the Maestro and Jan exchange a polite kiss-on-the-cheek farewell and then she takes Joey and settles her in the back seat. Beck is about to climb in after them, when Jan rests a hand on his shoulder.

'You are a brilliant pianist,' he says. 'Nerves can be controlled.'

If only it was just nerves.

'You do the Keverich name proud.'

Maybe it's dark, maybe Beck's deluded, but Jan's smile looks real.

Beck swallows. He can't ignore the poison, even if everyone else can. 'The ending. I completely screwed it.'

Jan shrugs. 'Mistakes do not cancel the worth of a performance. They encourage us to work harder, aim higher. Your mother and I had our fair share of catastrophes when we began performing, especially those particular études. Ask her someday.'

Um, no thanks.

Beck gets into the taxi and Jan grabs the door to close it. 'Good night. I look forward to tomorrow, Beck.' He shuts the taxi door.

And Beck is left waiting for his tragedy to begin.

CHAPTER 20

Beck's life is on pause, a broken string in the middle of a ferocious piece. She cannot touch him before he sees his uncle again, so the Maestro is wordless, motionless, like she's been carved from ivory and stone. She sees him into a taxi. Her tightly curled fists whisper promises of *later later later*.

Technically, Beck could tell the taxi to take him anywhere.

He doesn't.

He is too spineless. Or he wants to see Jan again?

Or maybe he's still perched on that wrong note, clutching it desperately, because when the chord fades, the Maestro will strike. Her silence won't last.

He walks the long driveway alone, feeling the restrictions of his new snug jeans. His backpack, stuffed with music and one of Joey's awful sandwiches, is slung over his shoulder. If his hair wasn't so crazy, if he didn't have the scuffed backpack, if he knew how to smile – maybe he'd look like he belonged here?

It takes an enormous length of time for someone to answer the doorbell. It's Audwin Denzel, his uncle's friend. He waves Beck in. 'Jan is upstairs. Come, *Sohn*.'

They bypass the ballroom and instead take the white-carpeted stairs to the second level. Then there's a twist of hallways and Denzel leaves him in the mouth of a music room – an actual *real* music room. It's flooded with light from floor-to-ceiling windows, and the walls are sky blue. And the piano? A white Steinway.

Just the thought of this guy having *two* grand pianos makes Beck weak.

Jan isn't there and the room is quiet. There are several bookshelves, a coffee table shaped like a quaver note and a white sofa that Beck's nearly too scared to sit on. But it's not like he's going to sit on the piano stool and tap a few notes while he waits. No thanks.

He rests his backpack on his lap – a shield? – and sits gingerly on the edge of the sofa. And waits.

Ten minutes?

Or a million years?

Finally Jan appears, a mug of steaming coffee in hand. He looks relaxed, casual, with jeans and a black pinstriped shirt, the impossible Keverich curls waxed down and an expensive watch on his wrist, loose and clinking against the mug.

He leans against the doorframe, sips his coffee and stares at Beck.

Are his eyes disappointed? Did Beck fail some sort of test? Great. He's messed up and he's been here all of ten minutes.

'I had a feeling,' Jan says. 'Now I'm sure.'

What? That Beck is uncultured in rich man's etiquette? Maybe he should've stood as his uncle entered? Maybe he shouldn't have sat on the snowy sofa?

Maybe he should've told the taxi to take him to the edge of the world and let him fall off.

Jan strides into the room. 'You hate it.'

'What?' Beck is failing this test, failing fast and hard.

'Someone who loves music, *breathes* music, wouldn't have been able to resist this piano. I've been waiting outside. You did not touch it or play it or even look at it.' Jan runs a hand along the grand's white side. 'You were too scared to put a fingerprint on it.'

Beck should probably say something. Defend himself? He sits stunned, mute.

'You sit as far from it as you can.'

Beck hadn't even *thought* about where he sat. He just – sat. So his uncle is analysing everything? This is stupid.

'Last night,' Jan goes on, his voice as crisp as new sheet music, 'you stayed on the verandah, again as far from the piano as you could be.'

'But Joey—'

Jan doesn't hear him. 'I wondered if it was stage fright. I said as much last night, to which you didn't blush or look embarrassed. You looked relieved. Because I hadn't *guessed*, had I?'

Stop.

This is a lie, isn't it? Where's the uncle with a smile as warm as hot chocolate and a laugh as bright as sunshine? This man is like the Maestro. Was yesterday all an act?

Beck should've known.

Jan slams his mug on the coffee table with an ominous crack. Black liquid sloshes over the sides.

Exactly like the Maestro.

How much of an idiot is Beck? Once upon a time, when her hands were perfect and her career rioting forward, the Maestro was probably all smiles and melodies too. Beck is a freaking moron. Why *didn't he see*?

And the worst part? He can't get away. He's not even sure he can find the front door of this monstrous house, and what would he do if he did? Walk halfway across the city to get home? He's trapped here, him and Jan and the piano.

'Did you make a mistake or are you the mistake?' Jan says.

Beck opens his mouth –

shuts it.

Jan's eyes harden and the next words are a roar. 'ANSWER ME.'

It's not *like* the Maestro, it *is* the Maestro. Beck shrinks into the sofa, his world melting. *Don't collapse, don't shrivel, don't let his words cut you open*. Why wasn't he born with the Keverich stone and steel?

'Both,' he says, because that's what the Maestro would want to hear.

His eyes close for a second, ready for insults to be hurled at his incompetent foolery. How he's no Keverich. How he's no pianist. How he is nothing.

But it doesn't come.

Jan sinks on to the sofa beside him, puts his head in his hands and rakes fingers viciously through his hair. Confused doesn't cover what Beck is feeling. He resists the urge to scoot away.

Jan pulls a crisply ironed handkerchief – who does that? Come on – from his pocket and mops up the spilt coffee, cursing softly about wasting good coffee and ruining the mug. Beck's brain spins, because that's not something the Maestro would think of. She leaves Beck to clean up the catastrophes.

'I should've used a coaster.' Jan gives Beck a sorry smile.

Is he messing with him? A cold sort of fury floods Beck's jaw. His hands knot into his backpack. What is *going on*?

Jan pushes the coffee away. 'You're not honest with me, Beethoven.'

'Beck.' He says it stiffly. He's torn between rage and embarrassment and terror here, but he's not going to be mocked. And his name is only a joke.

'Beck,' Jan amends. 'My apologies.'

Is this the Keverich curse? Psychotic mood swings?

'Be honest with me now,' Jan says. 'How much do you love the piano?' But as Beck opens his mouth, Jan holds up a finger, 'Ah. *Nein*. You are going to lie.'

'I'm not.' Beck's teeth grit.

Jan's eyebrow rises. 'Truly? I see your mother's words written all over your face. I see her behind your music choices. Those études? We played them as children because we were forced to make them perfect. Drove us both insane.' He shakes his head.

'I see her in your fear of mistakes. I see her everywhere about you. But, at the piano, I should see you.' He sighs and knits his fingers together. 'I apologise for the theatrics, though, my nephew. I needed to know you honestly.'

What?

'Does she hit you?'

Beck has lost all use of the human language.

'We are family,' Jan says. 'And I have waited years for your mother to contact me, to let me know where in this forsaken country she was *hiding*. She should never have left Germany. But, her shame ...' He trails off, but Beck knows.

How, after the stroke, his mother bypassed rehabilitation for the nerve damage in her hands. How she took him when he was just a toddler and left Germany without a goodbye. How she spent all her savings on the house. On the piano. How she couldn't bear to remember her past, so she cut it away like rot on an apple. How she wanted Beck to take up where she left off, so the world would be awed by the legacy of Ida Magdalena Keverich's prodigy son.

How he, unfortunately, was not a prodigy.

'I would have liked to be a father to you and Joey,' Jan says. 'But, you know your mother. She wanted to be alone until she was ready.' He turns on the sofa, faces Beck. 'So tell me. There is madness in the Keverich line, madness and fear and grief. But does she hit you?'

Bruised lips. Blood-streaked tiles. Hand-shaped bruises.

'I don't need rescuing,' Beck says, voice stretched thin. 'I'll save myself.'

He didn't know, until that moment, that it was true.

But it is.

Jan seems to read between the lines, because he nods and his eyes glow with a thin shred of satisfaction. '*Gut*. I am glad, Beck, I am glad. But I hope you will not refuse a little aid from someone who wants to be part of your life. And I apologise, again, for coming at you so violently. I know Ida's tempers. It appears they have not changed much, *ja*?'

Beck just shrugs.

He's being dissected and it's hard to breathe.

'I wish I could give Ida her music back. She is lost without it.' Jan's eyes cloud. 'But it is no excuse. I want to make your life better, my nephew. I want to make your existence exciting and spectacular.'

Beck would prefer an *OK* life. Where he goes to school and doesn't worry if there'll be dinner on the table and never touches a piano and maybe runs to August's house some nights to stargaze.

'What do you want, Beck? What do you want of this world?'

He checks to see if Jan is serious – and his uncle's gaze is level, expectant.

Great.

Beck screws his eyes shut and digs his thumb and forefinger into his forehead, massaging the ache. What *does* he want? He never used to think about it – until August shoved her way into his life. Now he wants so much that the cruel sharp ache of never being able to have it is unbearable.

He wants Joey to be safe. He wants to eat until he's stuffed. He wants to walk far, far away without a care in the world. He wants every string that ties him to the piano to snap. He wants the Maestro to say *well done*. He wants to write the music in his head, pages and pages of it, and never show it to a soul if he doesn't want to. He wants to *own* it.

He wants August. He wants his hand to fit into hers – all the time, whenever he wants. He wants to eat cake with her, listen to her teasing, laugh a little, carry her home from school when she forgets her shoes. He wants to kiss her a million times. And then once more. Because he can't put a number on how many times he wants to hold her, to feel safe next to her, to feel possibilities.

He doesn't want her as a friend.

He wants more.

She is the girl his songs are for.

None of these are answers he can give Jan, or even say aloud.

'I want to be a good pianist,' Beck says. 'I want to be a true Keverich.'

Disappointment crosses Jan's face and Beck feels ashamed.

'I thought you'd be honest with me, Beck.'

'I was,' Beck says, without thinking. 'I mean—'

'Do not worry.' Jan's smile is sad. 'I cannot demand your full trust when you barely know me. Unless—' He hesitates. 'Are you sure there is nothing else you want?'

What Beck Keverich wants most in the world is to cut off his own hands –

and

let a girl named August

teach him how to

smile.

'Yes,' says Beck, 'I do want something. I wrote a piece, a song –' *a confession of everything inside me* '– and I want to play it and record it.' He hesitates, his face burning. 'Please.'

He knows it's not what Jan means, but this is a chance, a request, and if Jan is claiming to be a fairy godmother, he can give Beck this.

'Who is it for?' Jan asks, but his tone is curious,

maybe even smudged with excitement.

'A – friend,' Beck says.

'The girl from the concert?'

Well, there goes that.

'August,' Beck says. Her name tastes like earth and sunshine. 'I know people have iPods and all that, but I want to make a CD.'

Jan's nod is slow at first, then vigorous. He bounces off the chair, enthusiasm sprouting like wings. 'I have a video camera. The quality will not be excellent, but the acoustics in this room are not bad. Good. We can do this. Right now.'

The worm of doubt has come – he hasn't even ever played the song before without stopping. And Jan will hear it.

'It's a mess,' Beck says, 'just – um, just know that the middle is rubbish, and I don't have the ending sorted so—'

'*Nein! Nein!*' Jan claps his hands together sharply. 'That is not how a creator talks about his music. I refuse to believe your music is wrong *or* rubbish. Someone has told you that and you believe it. Believe yourself.' He leans forward and taps Beck's chest. 'You said you would save yourself – do it.'

Jan gets the camera.

Beck gets hit with nerves and a thousand regrets.

As Jan sets up, Beck slides on to the piano seat

and gets a feel for it. The keys are always deeper on a grand, and he works them with the pedal and feels the rich, moody tone. His scribbles are at home, in the bin, crumpled under his pillow, scattered over the floor where Joey's drawn on them.

Beck closes his eyes and remembers.

'It is recording,' Jan says. 'Play whenever you are ready. *Viel Erfolg.*' *Good luck.*

Beck plays.

He stumbles. Seriously? His fingers are going to feel like worthless splinters today, of all days? The entire first movement comes out thick and messy. He stops, drops his hands into his lap, and hates himself.

'Maybe,' Jan says, his voice soft, 'you should play this for August. *For* her, not at her, not to her. *For* her. Play what August means to you. Play it as if you love her. As if you ...'

All Beck can hear is –

play

as if

you love

her.

So he does.

Jan, the camera, the room, even the oddness of the white piano, all shrink into microscopic factors. Beck's life is a flood of music, a kaleidoscope of blue and yellow and pink and orange, the smell of summer and rain. His fingers race away and he doesn't trip. Not once.

He plays for August.

And about her.

Then his fingers tremble, and the staccato bass line runs to the higher register, and he plays like he has the courage to kiss her when he absolutely doesn't.

He plays as if he loves her.

And some time while his heart breaks and skids across the universe like diamond beams of starlight, his thumb catches crookedly on a key and splits. Winter makes for dry skin and easily ripped nails. And now? His fingers dance bloody fingerprints over the white keys, as if the piano and Beck have finally become blood brothers,

and then the song is finished.

Beck puts his hands in his lap.

He leaves a smudge of blood on his new jeans and he totally just ruined a millionaire's piano.

'I'm sorry,' he says.

Is he crying?

He doesn't want to be crying.

Stop. *Stop.*

The recorder beeps as Jan shuts it off. Then he slides on to the stool next to Beck and they sit there, shoulders touching, admiring the reddened piano keys.

'I have never,' he says quietly, 'seen a student bleed over a piano. Oh, I've seen them bleed, but they always stop and coddle themselves because their music hurt them.'

'It always hurts me.'

'Ah.' Jan smiles. 'We are being honest now. But Beck, you – you wrote this. I – I am in awe.'

Beck puts pressure on his thumb before he, well, dies or something awkward.

Jan stares at him. 'If you can compose music like this, it is a sin for you to play from other composers. You are brilliant, Beethoven Keverich.'

And for once, Beck doesn't correct his name. He just swallows the words, lets them fill his heart, his lungs, his soul. It's not his name he hates. It's what people think it means.

Jan sounds like Beethoven and Beck are the same – not the dream versus the failure.

'Let me take you to Germany.' Jan's voice turns low, urgent. 'I am not your mother, I swear to you. You will have the best school, the best *Universität*. You are my nephew and brilliant and you do not deserve to be hidden.'

'I-I can't.'

It's like Jan didn't hear. 'I am often away on tours, but I have trusted friends who would check in on you while you get your bearings in the city and then, eventually, you'll have your own apartment. Your own life. I will give you the world and you will be my protégé.'

You could be away from the Maestro.

You could be free.

'I know there is this girl,' Jan says softly. 'August. And she makes you play like nothing in this world. But you deserve more. You deserve a life of promise, not fear. And if you decided to come with me but never play the piano again? So be it. I would not force you.'

It's like being beaten – but with hope instead of fists. Beck shuts his eyes, but a tear still frees itself and streaks down his face. He'd never see August again. And what about Joey? He couldn't leave her with the Maestro, for her life of glitter and gumboots to be cut from her soul while the piano took its place. The Maestro would never let her go. She'd never let Beck go either, if she knew Jan planned to be kind to him instead of chaining him to the piano. Beck could tell what she does to them. But she's his *mother* and she might still love them –

she might she might she might she—

Jan clears his throat. 'I don't expect your decision immediately—'

'I already know,' Beck says.

He can taste the blood in his mouth from when she'll hit him. He can feel the tremble in his bones as he stands between her and his baby sister.

When he opens his eyes, Jan's face is lit with expectation, excitement.

'No,' Beck says. 'I can't be your Beethoven.'

In his mind, it's like

cutting off his hands.

CHAPTER 21

He made the right choice. He did, *he did*.

Stop doubting yourself.

Beck climbs from the car – Jan insisted on driving him home – and forces himself to act casual, calm. But his insides are an ocean of regret and loss and confusion, because he should feel calm about staying. He should feel strong. He's no Cinderella to be rescued by magic.

He's a kid who writes music, who'd never leave his little sister behind.

He's a kid who's going to kiss a girl tonight. No more wishes, wonders, dreams. He's the one who'll act.

Jan lowers the electric window. 'Wait.'

Beck hesitates.

'You can change your mind.' Jan leans over and passes him a card. 'I am not sure this is *your* decision.'

Beck clutches the card like it might save him from drowning. 'It is. I'm sorry.'

Jan's eyes are doubtful, but he just nods and farewells in German. Then the car pulls out of the driveway and leaves the streets of broken glass and tired houses. Jan returns to his life of music and good food and expensive watches.

Beck walks towards the front door. He wishes he'd said more than *thank you*, because those two pathetic words hardly convey how much Jan has done. Beck is a good pianist. He's a better composer. He has a future.

He has promise.

The house is eerily quiet when Beck opens the door. He shrugs his backpack off his shoulder and checks that the CD is inside. He scrawled a title in black Sharpie and shoved it in an envelope. It's all he has for August. He leaves his bag at the door, because he expects he'll have to sneak out. As if the Maestro's going to grin and wave goodbye as he walks to August's for her birthday tonight.

The Maestro promised to break his hands.

But she won't.

Beck won't let her.

He feels a sharp electric thrill of confidence as he walks down the hall. The TV buzzes softly from the lounge and he heads for it, half thinking of the possibility of taking Joey with him to August's. She'd love the dogs. She'd love the food.

The lounge is empty.

Bright, perky cartoons dance on the screen and there are half-filled bowls of sultanas and biscuit crumbs where Joey would normally have had her snack.

She never leaves food lying around.

Beck backtracks to the kitchen. His shoes crunch crockery. He looks down.

The floor is covered with shards of smashed plates, ground to white dust in some places. It must be every plate in the house.

How did he not think this would happen?

Beck's stomach turns over. He treads carefully, plates biting into his shoes, and goes for Joey's room. Empty. Toys are scattered across the floor, but she always lives in a mess. Doesn't she? Does she? When was the last time Beck sat down and actually paid attention to Joey? He's been so swallowed by his own angst.

Don't go to your room. Go out the door. Go to August's. Go now.

He pushes his hands deep in his pockets and walks towards his room.

Somehow he knows.

His door is open.

'Joey?' Beck says, his voice hollow.

The Maestro sits on his bed, for once not trembling. She's rigid, wearing her nice pressed work clothes, as if she planned to go out today. Or as if she planned to go somewhere, anywhere – as if she planned to leave.

Joey sits on the piano stool, hunched, sniffling. Red fingerprints mark her cheek.

How dare the Maestro—

Beck takes two steps and he's at Joey's side, picking her up. Her short skinny arms go around his neck. But he doesn't know what to say. Does he ask? Does he walk out?

Jan's card burns in his pocket.

'You are not going to Germany?' the Maestro asks. It's so calm, so perfectly flat, that a shiver runs up Beck's spine.

He holds Joey tighter. 'No.'

'Then you will never be properly trained,' the Maestro says. 'The line of Keverich pianists ends with me.'

Except Beck is a pianist. Except Beck isn't worthless.

'Yes,' Beck says, his voice a hundred years old. 'I guess it does.'

She stands, unfolding like a stiff puppet with

rusted iron strings. Her hands are trembling, Beck sees now. She just had them bunched so tightly in fists that her fingernails have left gouges in her palms.

'So you do this to spite me?' she says.

Beck takes a deep breath. He unlatches Joey's hands from around his neck and, even when she whimpers, he puts her down and says quietly, 'Go watch TV, Jo.'

She drags her feet to the door and then hugs the wall, not moving.

Beck faces the Maestro. He's nearly as tall as her. When did that happen?

'*Nein*,' he says, accidentally using German to placate her when he means to stand up for himself for once. Habits are hard to break. 'I'm not going to do this any more.' Blood pounds in his ears. 'And you're never going to touch Joey again. Or me.' He feels dizzy with the effort to keep talking, to not back up as she comes closer, to not cower in case of a blow. 'I don't belong to you any more.'

You don't deserve anything from me.

I deserve a life away from you.

'Is that so?' the Maestro says, coolly. 'Yet here you are under my roof, wearing clothes I have bought you. *Dummes Kind*.' Stupid child. 'This is your piano that I spent every cent I owned on.'

But Beck didn't ask for that. He was too young

261

to even understand her nerve damage after her stroke, how it could have been helped with therapy, medication – but instead she bought a piano. *Not his choice*. Hers.

She keeps coming towards him and finally he steps back, pressed against the piano and the wall. The piano that built him, that destroyed him.

'I'm not playing any more,' Beck says as the piano digs into his back.

He should take Joey and leave, go to August's, get help – call the police. He wants to. Does he? This is his mother. She just – she just wanted him to be great. She's messed up and wrong and cruel as a knife, but she *wants him to be great*.

No. She *wants him to be her*.

'You will play the piano,' the Maestro says, her voice a symphony of darkness. 'You will play.'

'No.'

Beck stops cowering. He pulls himself tall, so he's nose-to-nose with her. He looks like her, he realises, when he doesn't back down or tremble – wild hair, height, steel bones and eyes that long for something out of reach.

Joey's voice is a hiccupping sob. 'Don't hurt him, Mummy.'

But the Maestro doesn't listen.

Does she ever listen?

'You will play,' she says, her voice spiralling

down a cold, callous hole.

He can barely get the words out. 'I don't – I don't want to live like this.'

Because he wants *to live*.

It happens fast, a storm that's brewed for days, a rusted nail about to give, a piano string too old, too frayed.

The punch catches Beck on the side of his head and sends him stumbling backwards into the piano. The keys howl. He does not.

Joey lets out a bubbling sob.

He wishes she didn't have to see this. He wishes Joey didn't have to think this is normal.

He straightens and pain throbs through his skull and there are marks on his hands where the piano keys bit. But he's barely upright before she shoves him again, her curses in thick German.

'Stop.' Is it a plea? Is it a demand?

When is he going to be more than a trembling semiquaver?

'Stop, *Mutter*. You can't – I'm not—'

'*HÖR AUF ZU REDEN.*' Stop talking.

She hits him again and he isn't ready for it, he still believes she'll stop and say sorry and promise she won't do it again. Every time she hits him, his stupid head thinks it'll be the last time. *She can't mean this.*

When is he going to realise she's built on regret

and smouldering hate?

'The piano is your legacy,' she screams.

'No it's *not*.' Beck shields his face with his arm. 'It's *yours*. It's your dream, not mine.' He tries to back away, but he's between a wall and the piano.

He's always been stuck here.

She hits out hard, fast, and blood trickles down his split cheek and it's stupid, he *knows* it's stupid, but all he can think of is how he can't turn up to August's like this again. She'll never get her song.

She'll think he didn't have the courage to come.

Which is true, isn't it? He's pathetic.

Stupid.

Worthless.

Schwachkopf. Moron.

'You break my heart,' the Maestro says, her voice cracked, crying. 'You are nothing when you should've been everything. Without the piano, there is nothing left of me. Nothing. You failed me. You failed everyone.' Her voice twists into a wail.

It's true. She's right. Beck fails school, life, Joey, August, Jan, the piano.

Fail – fail – fail.

'Beck! Beck!' Joey screams. She's a shadow behind the Maestro, trying to grab her mother's arm.

The Maestro's fingers twist into Beck's hair.

'You are my mistake, Beethoven.' She slams him into the piano.

His head connects with wood and paint and polish and for a second he sees nothing. It's like floating on the sea in a cardboard box. He's only dimly aware of Joey screaming. Of the Maestro smashing his head again. Of blood filling his ears. His eyes. Blood everywhere.

His eyes clear and he sees the piano, floating in a zigzag, smeared with his blood.

His voice is distorted, like he's yelling through a tunnel. 'Joey, call the police.'

'*NEIN*,' the Maestro screams. 'You are being punished! Or are you such a baby you cannot take it?'

He's being murdered.

He just has to hit back. Hit back. *Hit back.*

And be just like the Maestro?

He won't.

He refuses.

But he's struggling to know which way is up, where he is whoheiswhatisgoingon ...

A small body presses against his legs as he sags against the piano. She's between him and the Maestro.

'Don't, Mummy,' she says.

The Maestro backhands her.

It tosses Joey's little body halfway across the

room and she cracks into the wall with a sickening thud. She lies still. She can't be still. Is Beck screaming? He has to get to her, but the world is upside down and dripping blood.

He tries to get up but the Maestro hits him again and this time, when his head hits the piano, a sharp ringing splits his ears. He doesn't get up.

But his swollen lips move – in a whisper? Or a shout?

'You can't hurt your baby, *Mutter*. That's Joey. You can't hurt your baby Joey.' And he says it over and over

and over and over

and she doesn't hit him again.

When he cracks his swollen eyelids open, the Maestro is on her knees, pulling Joey's crumpled body into her arms and sobbing. Huge sobs. They shake her to the core of her bones.

Beck pulls himself to his feet and staggers out of the room. He's made out of cement and each step weighs a hundred kilos. He finds the phone in the kitchen and nearly drops it before he can get the number in. It takes him five tries to follow the line of wobbling digits on the card from his pocket.

Is the phone dead? He can't hear the dial tone.

Until faintly, like a tiny pinpoint of light, he hears someone pick up.

'I changed my mind,' he says, his voice thick.

'But Joey has to come.'

Did his uncle reply? Did he even dial the right number?

The phone tips from his hands and Beck sinks to the floor and cradles his throbbing head. It beats like a song. The song says goodbye.

CHAPTER 22

They ask him to say his name. Again and again. He can't make his tongue answer.

They shine a light in his eyes and say something about an ambulance. A stretcher? His mother? His head? Stay awake? Or go to sleep?

His mouth is still full of blood but he manages to say, 'I can't hear you.'

He gestures to his bloodied ears.

'I can't hear you. *I can't hear you.*' Does he scream or whisper?

He tells them his name, through swollen lips.

'Beethoven Keverich.'

CHAPTER 23

Technically Beck isn't allowed to go anywhere alone – safety reasons. Just until he gets used to his limitations.

But they are at his house, Jan and he, picking up anything he wants to take. Which is exactly nothing. His clothing is little more than rags, so Jan said they'll buy some before the flight this weekend. And he'll need advice for Joey's clothes because he's never bought for a little girl. He'll ask her favourite colour when they pick her up from the hospital this evening.

As for this house? Packing keepsakes? Is there anything special he wants to save?

Beck has nothing.

So he just walks out.

To August's house, obviously. Where else would he go? But how long has it been since he even talked to her? Over a week with his hospital stay? There's so much to say and he doesn't know where to begin. Does he start with hello?

Or goodbye?

Does he tell her he's leaving? For ever. As soon as they pick up Joey with the pink cast on her broken arm, they'll be on a one-way plane flight, her, Jan and him. Does he say he never has to see the Maestro again if he doesn't want? How she's signed over her children's custody to her brother. How Jan is still pressing charges against her. How Beck will have to testify and he can't think about that right now. He can't face it. Maybe he can't even *do it*.

Jan says they'll decide later.

Now is for leaving.

He could tell August how the Maestro kissed his forehead, even though he flinched away from her, and, cold and precise, she said, '*Ich liebe dich.*' *I love you.* And then she left the hospital and never looked back at all the things she had broken.

Does he wait till August asks about the yellow bruises on his face, the bandage on his left ear, or the stitches in his cheek? He should. No lies, this time.

While Jan tiptoed gingerly around the smashed house, Beck avoided his room with the bloodied piano and broken keys. He never has to play again, if he chooses.

But his music hasn't stopped. He's already scribbling new songs on the back of a hospital menu, his fingers dancing with notes on hallway walls as he walks because apparently composing is part of him and not likely to go away.

He walks slowly down his street – for the last time? – and tries not to jolt his aching limbs too much. His face feels tight beneath the stitches. That'll make her sad. After all this time, he still hasn't learnt to smile. Between his motley face and his new clothes, she won't even recognise him. Jeans that fit? A lined jacket? Shoes so new they squeak on shined floors? He's never felt so rich.

August's house looks the same – a relief. He nearly expects the world to be different since his life has changed so much. The only new addition is several chickens in the front yard that scatter as he walks to the front door. This time he won't lurk in her yard like some demented creeper. He'll knock. And if she's not home, he'll go and never come back.

He knocks.

The dogs are probably going crazy inside.

The door opens and two feet, with bare,

blackened soles and rainbow anklets, appear with a blast of cinnamon and flour. Her face is dusted with white and smudges of chocolate decorate her arms. Her lips are caught between a smile and a frown, but she doesn't hesitate. August throws her arms around his neck and presses her face into his collar. Her body shudders beneath him. What does he do? Maybe – just –

He returns the hug, holds her tight, rain hugging sunshine, and he remembers that she does care about him. She said so that night, when they ate the stars and she kissed him.

She opens her mouth, but he puts a finger to her lips. He wishes he could mentally transfer everything he wanted to say.

But that would be cheating.

Instead he says, 'Hi,' and pretends he's not crying.

She pretends she's not crying too.

He pulls the CD out of his back pocket and hesitates before he hands it to her. Can't take it back now. He accidentally wrote something precious into that song and sharing it is baring his soul. But he's OK with that.

This is August.

In thick Sharpie he's written:

FOR AUGUST: ALL THE THINGS I DIDN'T SAY.

She pulls him inside.

The dogs are all over him – her parents aren't home – and the house gives him a welcome hug of baking cinnamon biscuits and woodsmoke from their fire. August licks icing off her wrist as she scampers for her room, CD clutched desperately to her chest. Beck pauses to pat a dog, or nine.

He follows August slowly, half because he's drinking in her house for the last time and half because he doesn't want to see her face as she listens.

She sits cross-legged on her bed, battered laptop open before her as the song loads. She turns it up as loud as it can go and three of her cats leave the room. Beck is mildly offended.

Beck can feel the bass through the floorboards. Did he really play it that loud? He remembers the white piano and the blue room and Jan's excitement over discovering this is what Beck's good at. This is what he's made for.

It doesn't matter if it's nearly freezing outside, August's smile is lime and summer.

She's crying.

'That bad, huh?' he says.

She shoves his arm, always as physical and violent as a kitten.

Her lips open and don't pause and he can't get in a word edgewise until he leans across the bed and covers her mouth with his for the briefest heartbeat of a second. Then he scoots so he sits beside her, their thighs touching, and he tilts his right ear towards her.

He has to stop pretending. He has to talk normally. He can't let the tremor into his voice. This is August and he doesn't have to pretend, but he'd like her last memory of him to be a creator of dancing notes not a crying boy.

'If you talk really loud to my right side,' he says, husky, 'I'll be able to hear.'

At least the Maestro didn't break his hands.

The Maestro took his hearing. Not all of it. And a specialist says there are options to look into and Jan promises they will in Germany. And for now? Beck doesn't even mind that much. He's not missing anything. He has a ridiculous amount of music in his head now that it's all he can hear.

'... no ... how can ... Beck ...' is all he gets from August.

He tells her to slow down, lean in, speak clearly. She has to stop crying for that, so she takes a second to swallow and straighten her shoulders and tuck a stray strand of hair behind her ear.

'The song says it all,' Beck says, his voice a garble to him but hopefully clear for her. 'Everything I ever thought about you. And more.' *Like what you mean to me.* 'And a bit of an

274

apology. I missed your birthday.'

She rolls her eyes. 'Like that is ... and ... matters.'

'I tried to capture you in the music,' he says, feeling like an idiot. He's not an artist. This isn't a painting.

'You caught me,' she says. 'And you with the ... love it.'

He hopes he didn't make it up. He hopes she *loves it*.

'I'm going to Germany.' Beck feels the room shrink and wither. August's body stiffens beside him. 'Joey and me. I'm going to write a million songs.'

'For ever?' She swipes her eyes with her knuckles and keeps her back straight, her posture undefeated. She frowns a little but nods. 'I always wanted to see Germany.'

His smile is all a mess. 'I don't – August. I ...'

'When I finish school, I ... backpack the world,' August says. 'First stop is apparently Germany.' She smiles, but it doesn't reach her eyes.

I'll miss you, Beck wants to say.

He stares at her feet.

He doesn't want this to be the end of August Frey, the girl who prompted him to save his life. He doesn't want this to be the last song he writes for her or the last time he dusts flour off her cheek with his thumb or the last time he smells her kiwi

275

fruit shampoo or gets lost in her ocean eyes.

'I think,' Beck says, 'that I like you quite a lot, August Frey.'

'Likewise, Beethoven Keverich,' she says fiercely.

She slips her small, warm hand into his trembling one and their fingers knot. How come they have to fit so perfectly, so briefly?

Please don't let her forget him.

Did he say that out loud?

'Do you think I'm going to forget you?' she says, her lips close to his ear. 'I'll listen to … song on repeat until … demand you write me a sequel.'

'I'll write you an entire symphony if you ask.'

He'll write her enough songs to cover the entire world.

'A very loud symphony,' August says. 'And when a freaking huge German orchestra plays this … a front-row seat.'

'I'm sorry it's not perfect, though,' Beck says. 'I totally made mistakes—'

'Oh stop it.' She faces him, speaking clearly, and he hears her this time. 'You are worth more than a thousand perfect notes.'

And finally, his hands stop
trembling.

ACKNOWLEDGEMENTS

It's not easy to write acknowledgements when you're clutching your own book and whispering, 'Look, it's a real book!' which is basically what I'm doing all the time now. I'm so ridiculously pleased my years and years of words and wishes are now book-shaped and I can share them with you instead of hoarding them in a drawer. An overwhelming amount of thanks goes:

To my super agent, Polly Nolan, who is endlessly fantastic and has a magical way of making my stories a hundred times better. Forever grateful to work with you.

To my editors, Megan Larkin and Rosalind McIntosh, champions of my book and a hundred thank-yous are owed! And to the brilliant Orchard team for making *A Thousand Perfect Notes* absolutely (I can't help myself) *perfect*.

To Maraia Bonsignore and Sebastian Lecher for help with my translations. My characters wouldn't be able to yell in German without you. I'm so grateful. (And Maraia! Thank you for our endless texts and your endless encouragement.)

To Emily Mead, your feedback is invaluable and you've survived so many bad drafts and decoded so many typos. You're truly incredible.

To all those who tirelessly cheered for me through my blog, paperfury.com!

To my parents, for giving me books and then giving me more books because I finished the first ones too fast. You have created a book monster, I hope you're proud. Thank you for taking my work seriously even back when I was small(er) and stapling my books together myself while listening to Beethoven symphonies on repeat.

I'm so grateful you're all part of my story.

Don't miss the next book by C.G. Drews:

THE BOY WHO STEALS HOUSES

Read on for a sneak peek …

If it hadn't been so dark and if his fingers hadn't been so stiff with dried blood, he could've picked the lock in thirty-eight seconds.

Sammy Lou takes pride in that record. It's one of the few things he *can* take pride in, considering his life consists of charming locks, pockets full of stolen coins, broken shoelaces, and an ache in his stomach that could be hunger or loneliness.

Probably hunger.

He should be used to being alone by now.

He just needs to crack this freaking lock before someone sees and calls the cops. The house has been empty for days – so says the mouldering newspaper on the driveway, the closed curtains, the lack of lights at night. He knows. He's watched.

And now he's been at this lock for over two minutes. His palms go slick with sweat and the dried blood dampens and slips between his knuckles. His lock picks, a gift from his brother and usually an extension of Sam's thin and nimble fingers, feel too thick. Too slow.

He can't get caught.

He's been breaking into houses for over a year now.

He can't get caught.

One of his lock picks gets jammed and he whispers a curse. He wriggles it free, but his heart thunders and seconds tick by too fast, so he abandons the lock and melts back into the shadows. There's always another way.

He slips around the house, undone shoelaces slapping his ankles. The house is old bricks, the windows cloistered with drawn blinds. It's harder to see back here, with a tall fence blocking the moonlight. But a woodpile sits under a small window – no security screens – and it whispers welcome.

Sam dumps his backpack on the grass and scales the woodpile, placing each foot and hand gingerly so he doesn't end up underneath an avalanche of split logs. He's sore enough as is, thanks. His hands trace the small bathroom window and for once he's pleased he skipped out on the growth spurts regular fifteen-year-old boys encounter. He's a year off for his age. Maybe two. Looking small and pathetic usually works to his advantage though, plus it turns tight windows and poky corners into opportunities.

Half balancing, half hugging the wall, Sam fiddles with the lock while the woodpile gives an ominous groan and shifts beneath him.

Things this family is good at: locking their house.

Things they suck at: stacking wood into a sturdy pile.

If this doesn't work, he'll have to—

'You could always break it.'

Sam's heart leaps about forty feet in the air – and unfortunately his feet follow. For a second he scrabbles to grip the wall, bricks ripping his fingertips, and then he loses balance and tumbles backwards. The lock picks go flying into the darkness.

At least there's not far to fall.

At least the woodpile doesn't tip over too.

At least, Sam thinks, still on his back and staring up at a silhouette smudged against the stars, it's only his brother.

For a second Sam just lies there while the dewy grass soaks his back and he waits for his heart to migrate back down from his throat.

'Dammit, Avery,' Sam says.

'I didn't bring a hammer.' Avery pulls his phone out of his pocket and flips the torch app on and shines it straight in Sam's eyes. 'But we could use a rock or, like, your head since it's hard and ugly enough.' He gives the tiniest breath of a laugh, but follows quickly with, 'That was a joke. I was joking. You can tell it's a joke, right?'

Sam wasn't prepared for this tonight. Interruptions and complications and—

Avery.

And Avery wouldn't show up unless—

'Is something wrong?' Sam says, shielding his eyes from the glare. 'Are you hurt or in trouble or …' His pulse quickens. 'You're OK?'

'What?' Avery blinks, confused. 'Yeah, I'm fine.'

Sam didn't realise, until the *I'm fine* comes, how tight his chest is. How shaky his hands suddenly are. He has to close his eyes a minute and fumble for a thin grip on calm. It's fine. Avery's fine. Sam scrambles up and snaps, 'Turn that light off.'

He doesn't mean to snap. It's just that rush of panic for nothing.

'You're mad?' Avery tries to hold the phone out of Sam's reach, but it's a wasted effort since he's all elbows and sharp jawlines and a pointy elfish face like he skipped the effort of growing too, and Sam could just snatch it off him.

'I'm about to be really mad.' Sam's teeth clench. 'Turn it off or I'll smack you into the middle of next week.'

Avery frowns but turns the light off.

Sam's lost his night vision now. His ears strain, but doesn't catch any movement or whispers. Or sirens. He's not caught.

'I could get you a phone.' Avery rocks on his heels. 'That would fix everything.'

Of course it would, Avery. A phone would fix the fact that Sam is a house thief in clothes he stole from a bin at a second-hand store, who needed a haircut months ago, with skin tight against his ribs like a tally of all the meals he's missed.

His fingers curl into fists. Sticky with blood. It's all bluff anyway because he'd never hit Avery. In fact it's the opposite. Sam spends his life hitting the world and smoothing over the rusty corners so Avery won't fall and hurt himself.

'I wouldn't need you to fix stuff,' Sam says, the barest frustrated tremble in his voice, 'if you'd stop ruining everything.'